FEISTY RED

THREE CHICKS BREWERY #2

STACEY KENNEDY

For kick-ass single moms!

CONTENT WARNING

References to physical abuse and emotional trauma.

Stacey Kennedy

www.staceykennedy.com

Edited by Lexi Smail

Copy Edited by Monica Bogza

Cover Design by Regina Wamba

Manufactured in Canada

1

"**M**ama, I don't want to go."

Clara Carter didn't think six words could rip her heart out, but she felt the pain in her chest as she hid behind the curtain of her reddish-brown hair. Every little bit of her soul wanted to reach out and grab her six-year-old son, Mason, and keep him safe in her arms, but today wasn't about her. Today was about Mason and the fact that his safe, sheltered life wasn't so safe or sheltered anymore. Sullivan Keene, Mason's birth father and the man who vanished from Clara's life nearly seven years ago had come back to town.

Standing in her childhood home, where her grandparents had raised her, she thought nothing could ever touch Mason or her. Not in this house, where so much loved lived. Mason had only asked once about his birth father, and Clara had given the vaguest honest answer she could: *Sometimes, people can't be in our lives. We miss them. We wonder what they're doing and where they are, but sometimes, it's better for us if they stay away.* Since then, Mason had never asked again. Clara amounted that to the love from her family, who'd filled that void for Mason. Instead of Father's Day, they had Auntie's Day. Mason had never missed his father, because Sullivan simply didn't exist in Mason's young world. Even now, all around her were reminders of the love in this house. Its hardwood floors creaked, worn from a wonderful life. The distressed furniture, cozy and soft from many nights spent around the fire. But that comfortable bubble Clara had been living in shook with trepidation as she faced Mason again. Her son's sandy-brown eyebrows furrowed over stormy, light green eyes. She cupped his chubby face. "Don't be silly. You're going to stay with Penelope tonight." Penelope, Clara's cousin who'd moved to River Rock last Christmas, was now Mason's favorite person.

He stomped his foot, little hands fisted at his sides. "I don't wanna sleep over. I never do that."

Clara restrained her cringe. She didn't need the reminder that today was different from any other day. She felt unsteady, all the unknowns piling up on her shoulders. Determined to not drag this out, she moved to the staircase and grabbed his red backpack for school, along with another bag filled with his pajamas, toiletries, and clothes for tomorrow. "You'll have so much fun, and you don't want to hurt Penelope's feelings. She's very excited to have you overnight."

The crunching of gravel caught Clara's attention, and before Mason could object further, she opened the front door. He dug his heels in a little as she gently guided him outside.

When the car rolled to a stop next to the porch steps, the passenger-side window slid down. Penelope's warm green eyes landed on the very grumpy Mason. Her long, choco-late-brown hair was pulled into a side braid today, her light makeup was spot on, and Penelope's smile instantly brightened their morning. "I hear we're getting pizza tonight, going for ice cream, and watching a Spiderman movie." When Mason didn't move an inch and his frown deepened, Penelope slowly lifted a bag. "Oh, and eating candy too."

Clara didn't know her kid could move that fast. Mason beelined for the car.

"Bye, Mama," he called, fastening his seat belt.

The tightness strangling Clara's chest eased slightly as Penelope winked. "We'll be good for tonight."

Clara folded her arms in a terrible attempt to warm her bones. "Thanks for watching him overnight. I really appreciate it." Depending on people was hard. Sometimes impossible. Penelope made it easy. "He needs to be dropped off at school for eight o'clock, both today and tomorrow. Pick up today is at three."

"No problem," Penelope replied then tickled Mason, sending him into a fit of laughter. "You know I love any time I can get with this cutie."

They said quick goodbyes before Mason could change his mind, and soon, his sweet laughter faded as Penelope drove down the long driveway. The world felt like it began falling down on Clara's head. She wanted to run and hide so nothing could fracture the happy life she had created for him. But that was not rational, and she wouldn't let her emotions run wild today.

"I've got exactly what you need," a voice broke through the silence.

Clara glanced behind her, finding the youngest Carter sister standing in the doorway. Maisie was everything Clara wasn't. A free spirit. Wild. Adventurous. Her dark blue eyes always held a mischievous glint, her dirty-blond hair was unruly, and most days, she had paint somewhere on her body. She was the creative brains of Three Chicks Brewery, the company she and her two sisters had built from the ground up after Pops, their grandfather, passed away and left them the Colonial house, along with the barn that now housed the brewery. Even Penelope had a stake in the company now, handling the beer tours that came through. Which allowed Maisie's position to become a part-time job as she was planning on opening an art studio in town. "What do you have for me?" Clara asked for clarification.

Maisie raised her arm, revealing a shot glass. "Necessary fuel for today."

Only Maisie would think it appropriate to down what looked like whiskey at a quarter to eight in the morning. Clara envied Maisie's life, full of passion with her new fiancé, Hayes, and how every one of her dreams had come true. Maisie deserved that, but Clara didn't have the luxury of chasing her happily ever after. She had Mason. And while the day ahead felt unbearable, this was the day they'd been waiting for since they opened the brewery.

After hard months of grueling work, beer tours, and brewery awards, they finally got a shot at a distributor. With the distributor's help, they could put their top beer, Foxy Diva, into every bar and restaurant in North America. Reminded of all the responsibilities weighing heavily on her, Clara figured a little help to ease her nerves wouldn't hurt. She took the shot glass and downed the whiskey, shutting her eyes as the warmth of the liquid burned down her throat.

"It's understandable if you're feeling out of sorts right now."

Clara handed Maisie the empty shot glass. "I'm not feeling out of sorts. I know exactly what I'm doing." Maybe if she said that a hundred more times, she'd believe it too.

Obviously not believing her sister, Maisie gave a little

shrug. "Okay, then, what's the plan besides looking about ready to crawl out of your skin?"

Clara rolled her eyes. "I'm fine, Maisie. The plan is simple: impress the distributor." Only problem? The distributor was Sullivan's uncle, Ronnie. Clara hadn't known Sullivan was coming back to town. And she'd nearly had the wind knocked out of her when she arrived for a meeting with Ronnie and saw Sullivan sitting at the table too.

"Yes, of course, we're going to impress the hell out of Ronnie," Maisie said, quirking up her lips. "But let's not forget you're also going to see the man you thought you'd marry and who cruelly left you behind and broke your heart."

Clara gave the empty shot glass another look. Maybe she needed more than one to get through today. "What are you getting at, Maisie? Do you want me to cry or something?"

Maisie scanned Clara's face a little too closely. "No, I don't want you to cry. But I think you need to talk about this. Mason's birth father is back in town. And you have hardly said anything about it. What's the plan? Hiding Mason away until Sullivan leaves town again?"

Sounded good to Clara. Her stomach nearly heaved her breakfast out onto the old wooden porch. It all seemed like a bad dream she had to wake up from. When Sullivan left River Rock to play Major League Baseball, she never expected to see him again. *Ever.* "There is no plan," she finally admitted. "I only know that, right now, Mason not being here is safer for him. I can't take a wrong step here. I need to see where Sullivan is at emotionally before I even think about telling him about Mason." She'd tried once to tell Sullivan about Mason when she first found out she was pregnant. He didn't answer the phone. An unknown woman did, with the sound of a laughing Sullivan in the background. Clara never called back, and he never returned her call.

That was nearly seven years ago.

Maisie's look turned measured. Her voice softened. "One day, Mason is going to want to know who his father is. What are you going to say?"

"I've always been honest with Mason, and I will always be honest with him. When he asks for the truth, I'll tell him. But for as long as I can, I will protect him. He needs stability and love, not chaos and heartbreak." And that's all Sullivan knew how to do. She understood, to an extent. He had his own dark past. His own pain. But considering the only reason Sullivan was back in town was because he was suspended for causing a bar fight, Clara didn't expect much had changed. She felt more protective of Mason than ever. Wanting to run from this conversation, she turned to head down the porch steps, when a sudden *bang* echoed across the air. She whirled back to Maisie. "You heard that, right?"

"I heard that," Maisie said, eyes wide.

Hoping to hell the brewery wasn't about to explode, Clara took off, running toward the barn and what she assumed was a broken keg. On the weekends, the parking lot was full of cars from the brewery tours. Today, the only person in the barn was the middle Carter sister, Amelia, the Brewmaster, who'd spent the night brewing a new batch of their top beer, Foxy Diva.

"Amelia," Clara called, running through the double doors of the barn.

She skidded to a halt as she spotted her sister standing on the ladder next to a metal keg. Amelia's blue eyes looked as concerned as Clara felt. She had her long ginger-colored hair pulled up into a messy bun. Her freckle-covered nose was scrunched. "Clara," she yelled, hands extended in front of her.

Another loud *crash* followed by a *whooshing* sound had Clara instantly regretting entering the barn. A keg was tipping over, and the contents of spent barley were heading straight for her.

The gunk hit her like a brick wall. She felt the goop begin to slide down her face and land on the ground with a *splat.*

"Oh, my God, Clara..." Amelia slapped a hand over her mouth.

"I'm going to..." Clara spit the disgusting stuff out of her mouth. She looked down and surveyed the damage. Head to toe, sludge that smelled slightly sour covered her. She glanced back to Amelia and promised, "Kill you."

Amelia's hand slowly lowered, and her mouth quivered.

"Don't you even think about it," Clara warned.

Behind her shoulder, Maisie snickered.

"Don't," Clara snapped to her too.

A beat. Then both of her traitorous sisters burst into a fit of laughter.

Until a smooth voice said, "I see some things haven't changed at all."

Clara cursed her life. Even if she didn't want to, she glanced behind her and faced the very reason her lungs could barely get air today. Six foot two and a wall of hard muscle greeted her. A dark-haired hottie, professional baseball player, and baby daddy who didn't know about said baby, Sullivan Keene watched her with devastating, warm green eyes.

For all of her stress and worry about this moment, the panic and anger didn't come. No, something worse happened. Something unthinkable. Her heart fluttered.

2

Sullivan Keene did two things well.

One, play baseball. The Red Sox had scouted him in college. His fast-pitch had a 100.6 mile per hour average with a velocity of 2,530 average spin rate. Over the last season, his cutter earned him an insane run of 124 strikeouts.

The second thing he did well? Fuck up epically. His last disastrous decision had been a bar fight that ended up on the cover of a tabloid magazine and earned him a month-long suspension. That night had been the breaking point when Sullivan knew his life had to change. The last time he'd gotten into a blackout rage and fought in a bar was before he left River Rock. He had no doubt the recent death of his father a few months back was the root cause for this latest fight. So, when he'd been handed the suspension, instead of staying in Boston, or sticking close to Fort Myer where the team trained, he came back in River Rock in hopes of facing the trauma of his past. Trauma he hadn't thought about in a long time. Trauma that had stayed buried until the passing of his father.

But the greatest thing he'd ever fucked up was staring at him with captivating deep-blue eyes and pink pouty lips. Seven years ago, he'd been full of demons he didn't want touching her. Now, all that was left was regret. After Sullivan landed at the airport, he passed through Denver to see his uncle Ronnie before coming to River Rock and the apartment he rented for the month. When he heard from his uncle that Clara was coming into Denver for a meeting, Sullivan invited himself to join. Because he knew, to move on for good, he didn't only need to make peace with the tumultuous relationship he'd had with his father, but with Clara too.

He had thought of her often over the years, and he'd done his best to push her from his mind. But one look into those pretty eyes, and he knew, without a doubt in his mind, that he loved her as much now as on the day he'd left her. Admittedly, she seemed different. There was a hardness on her face he didn't remember, and her eyes were wary, cautious. Her reddish-brown hair was tightly pulled in a ponytail, and that tightness matched the line of her mouth. While all of that was new and jarring, some things hadn't changed. She could still fill out a pair of jeans like no other woman, and she could hold his attention until he couldn't see a damn thing but her. And with her soaked in sludge from head to toe, her shirt was skin-tight, revealing the body of a woman, not the twenty-one-year-old he'd walked out on.

"Sullivan," Clara said, voice clipped.

His gut tightened at his name on her tongue. She'd barely acknowledged him yesterday when he saw her, only determined to land a contract with his uncle. Now she looked right at him, and his world narrowed on entirely on her. "Hey, Slugger."

Her eyes narrowed at the nickname he'd always called her. Whatever Clara did, she'd hit it out of the park. "Don't call me that," she said, carefully calm. Her eyes lied, though; they blinked twice, warmth swirling in their depths. To put him in his place, her gaze skipped past him, like he didn't matter much, and fell to his uncle. "I'm really sorry about this, Ronnie. I'll need a few minutes to get cleaned up. Is it all right if Maisie shows you around the property?"

Sullivan had only heard about the Carter sisters' new venture yesterday from his uncle. He'd been as surprised to learn of their growing brewery as he was impressed by the presentation she put on in his uncle's conference room. Having found the perfect excuse to see Clara at that meeting, and hoping he got her to pause long enough so they could talk, he asked his uncle if he could come along for today's visit. Luckily, his uncle had obliged him. Sullivan looked to the side, finding his uncle frowning at Clara.

"Is everything all right?" Ronnie asked, surveying the damage.

Clara nodded and spit out more of the sludge, wiping her mouth with the back of her hand. "Yes, everything is fine. This doesn't happen often. Ever, actually. Excuse me for one quick sec." Fierce, like the Clara he remembered, she kept her eyes and chin up, striding out of the barn.

"Ronnie," Maisie quickly said in Clara's absence, all amusement now gone from her face. "Let's start at the back of the brewery, and we can work our way up."

"Excellent," his uncle said. He looked nothing like Sullivan's father, Kurtis. Ronnie had the Keenes' light green eyes but, at five foot seven, was shorter than Kurtis' and Sullivan's six foot two. Ronnie was also bald, whereas Sullivan had his grandmother's light brown hair.

Sullivan went to follow behind the group, amazed at

how grown up the Carter sisters were. When he'd seen them last, they were awkward teenagers. He wasn't sure how he felt about that. Time had gone by, so much time. And yet, there he was, back in River Rock, no longer running from his demons, but determined to face them.

As he headed past Amelia, who gave him a wave, his cell phone rang in his pocket. He grabbed it. One look at the screen revealed it was his agent. "I need to take this," he told his uncle.

"Yeah, yeah," Ronnie said, waving him off and focusing back on Maisie, who was talking about beer tours and events.

Sullivan turned away and pressed the phone to his ear. "What's up, Marco?"

"Not much here." Marco had represented Sullivan since Sullivan was scouted. "How are things out in the middle of nowhere?"

"Quiet," Sullivan answered, kicking up some gravel as he left the barn.

Marco gave a dry laugh. "I can only imagine. Listen, I talked to Coach Hale a few minutes ago."

"Yeah, what's he saying?" He could still hear the coach's roar in the locker room as he read the headline: Sullivan Keene hits hard at the club! The only thing he'd hit hard was that asshole's face. Luckily for Sullivan, he hadn't had a bat that night. He wasn't sure what he would have done with it. He'd only ever snapped like that once, and that was the driving reason he left River Rock and Clara behind.

"It's simple, Sullivan," Marco answered. "Take this month; you've got to get your head straight. Frederick"—the owner of the team—"is coming down hard on Coach Hale about how this makes the team look. This is your last shot. One more fuck up, and you're done."

He got it. He'd had a few articles written about him in the tabloids over the last few months. None of them put him in the best light. "Yeah, I got it."

Marco hesitated. "They're in their rights to do this, Sullivan, under your contract."

"I know."

"You got this. Right? I don't have to worry about you?"

"Yeah, I got this. See you in a month." Sullivan ended the call, not having more to say than that. He was drowning when he should have been gliding through the water. His game was on point. But something wasn't right in his head, and Sullivan had been pushing that down and down, and with his career on the line, something had to change.

A *bang* had him glancing over his shoulder to find the front screen door slamming shut behind Clara as she left the house. Sullivan watched her closely and the way she held his gaze like she told herself she had to. He didn't fault her there. She had something to prove to him, and he'd let her prove it. She deserved far better than the shit he'd given her. "All cleaned up?" he finally asked, breaking the heavy silence.

Freshly dressed in jeans and a blouse that somehow brightened the blue in her eyes, she stared at him coldly. It looked forced. He understood why, though. He vividly remembered how she tasted, how she looked when she smiled lovingly at him. He remembered it all. But she wanted to show him she no longer felt that way. She stopped in front of him, giving him a thorough once-over. "You look good, Sullivan. Different, but good."

"Different, how?"

She tilted her head, analyzing him in a way no other woman had analyzed him. Clara knew him. All his faults. All his weaknesses. All his pain. "Strong...old."

He lifted a brow at her. "I look old?"

"Yup." She strode by him.

He stared after her like a damn fool. "It's only been seven years since I've seen you. I can't look *that* old."

"Just shy of seven," she answered, heading off to the barn.

Of course, this gave him a fantastic view of her spectacular ass. An ass he had no business looking at. He forced his eyes up. "Wait up," he called then jogged to catch up to her.

When she finally reached the barn, she turned back to him. "Fine. You look *older*. Is that a better choice of word? I've never known you to be the sensitive type, Sullivan."

He wasn't the sensitive type. Yet, she was getting right under his skin. "I've never known you to be so outspoken, Clara."

She gave him a leveled look. "People change."

"Yeah, they do." And that's exactly what had brought him there. To her. To face the damage he'd done in hopes of finding peace. "I heard about Pops' passing. I'm sorry you lost him. I know how close you were." Clara's grandfather had been good people. Sullivan wouldn't bother with an apology for not calling or coming to the funeral. He didn't have a good excuse.

Her eyes saddened for a moment, and her pace slowed. "Pops would have loved to see the brewery flourish, so how about we go and find the others?"

For a split second, in her sadness, he saw the old Clara. *His Clara*. He didn't know what motivated him to grab her hand, stopping her, but his fingers soon wrapped around hers. Her gaze snapped to his, and she jerked away. "Do not touch me, Sullivan."

He shoved his hands into his pockets. "I'm sorry. I just..." *Want to apologize. Want to explain. Want to fix all this.*

"What *you* want is not relevant here," she snapped, striding away.

Knowing he deserved that, he blew out a long breath and followed her into the barn. Rows of tanks lined the old building, which admittedly, didn't even look all that old anymore. The barnwood had been stripped and re-stained, the floors coated with new lacquer.

"As you can see, we're set up to handle the quantity needed for distribution," Amelia said as Maisie led Ronnie out from the back. Amelia followed then gestured to her right. "We've got tons of room to expand."

Ronnie stopped and glanced around with an unreadable look. Truth was, Sullivan wasn't close to his uncle. But being the only family he had left, they kept in touch over the years with a phone call on holidays and birthdays.

"I'm liking what I see," Ronnie eventually said. He looked around once more, studying the impressive space. "Give me a couple days to examine your proposal and talk with the team about a plan."

Clara gave a very polite smile. "We look forward to hearing from you."

Sullivan nearly snorted. They both knew they had something great here that would benefit them both. He kept the thought to himself as Ronnie said his final goodbyes. When his uncle was heading back to his truck, Sullivan said to Amelia and Maisie, "It's hard to believe you're the two little ankle bitters I used to know." They were women now, but he could still see the mischievous glint in Maisie's eyes and the warm affection on Amelia's face.

"Well..." Maisie replied. "That's what happens when someone leaves and never comes back."

He deserved the dig. "You're right, it does." He sank his hands into his pockets, realizing he had two more people to make amends with. Not that he was surprised, the Carter sisters were close, especially Clara and Amelia. "I hear congratulations are in order." Maisie had just become engaged to Sullivan's old buddy Hayes.

An honest smile crossed her face. "Thanks. Hayes and I are very happy."

"Sullivan," Ronnie called.

Looking over his shoulder, he found his uncle frowning, waving him forward. Turning back to the sisters, he said, "It's really good to see you're all doing so well."

"How long are you in town?" Amelia asked, and the question didn't feel friendly.

"A month."

A month too long, Amelia's expression screamed at him.

Firmly put in his place, and more determined than ever to fix the hurt and damage he'd done to this family, he gave a firm nod. "I hope this new venture works out for you all. Take care."

No one said goodbye to him, or even responded with niceties. They all watched him with crossed arms and matching frowns.

He walked away then, feeling their hard stares burning into the back of his head. He'd make this right. And luckily, he had a month to do it.

3

Hours after Sullivan left, Clara still couldn't shake the tension nearly suffocating her. A month? Sullivan planned to stay a month? She didn't know how she could possibly keep Mason out of sight for that long. However, she also knew Sullivan, wholly and completely, and she knew he wouldn't stay that long in River Rock. The moment things got hard and he was forced to face all the reasons that had made him leave before, he'd book it again. All she needed to do was keep Mason close until that happened. She knew all too well what it felt like to be loved by Sullivan. It was an all-consuming thing, and she also knew what it felt like to have all that ripped away because he couldn't emotionally deal with it. She didn't know why he was here to ride out his suspension, and she didn't particularly care. Mason's well-being was her only concern. She wanted to go to her son and hold him close, but she needed the night to clear her head and to remind her fluttering heart that her love for the Sullivan she once knew died the day he left River Rock.

When she had left her sisters wrapping up their workday, she headed for her bedroom. The space was practical but comfortable. She'd had the double bed for more years than she dared count. The old, worn beige-and-white quilt was made by her grandmother when Clara was twelve, and she had picked up the refurbished antique white furniture at a flea market and repainted it herself. Clara sat on her bed and pulled out the letter left for her in Pops' will.

"WE ARE WHAT WE PRETEND TO BE, SO WE MUST BE CAREFUL WHAT WE PRETEND TO BE." KURT VONNEGUT JR.

Their grandfather left letters for both of her sisters too, though Clara had never asked if he'd left a confusing quote for them as well. Two years had passed now since their Pops left this world, and Clara knew as much about the quote as she did the day she opened the envelope at the reading of his will. She exhaled the confusion from her head, wishing he was there to explain it all. Pops was a wise man, full of useless knowledge in addition to the important stuff. Somewhere in this quote, Clara knew she'd find the comfort she needed in life; she just hadn't got there yet.

"Clara," Amelia called from downstairs.

She hurried off the bed, folding up the letter and sticking it back in her nightstand. When she made it to the staircase, she found Amelia standing at the bottom with a large pitcher full of margarita mix. "Seriously, why do you both keep feeding me booze? Do I look like I need a drink that badly?"

Amelia smiled. "Yup."

"Great," Clara muttered, trotting down the staircase. When she entered the kitchen after Amelia, she immediately spotted Maisie sitting around the old, worn oak kitchen table and inhaled the citrusy scent of limes. Back in the day, family meetings were held here with their grandparents. The tradition had lived on, and there was something about the table that always felt safe. "I'm okay, you know," Clara said to her sisters. "You don't need to stay," she said to Maisie.

Maisie was moving her stuff out of the house in a couple of days to live with Hayes in a gorgeous home by the creek. Her youngest sister smiled. "Please, like I could pass up margaritas."

Clara forced a smile and took her seat across from Maisie. When times got tough, some people chatted over coffee, some over chocolate, the Carter sisters drank margaritas. And usually, a lot of them.

Amelia began pouring the drink mix into the margarita glasses and asked, "So, thoughts on today?"

Maisie shrugged. "I think it went well with Ronnie. He seemed impressed by the brewery."

"I agree it went well," Clara added. "Now we just wait to see what kind of contract he offers us."

"But we'll take it, right?" Amelia asked, finishing up with the last glass. "No matter what it is."

"We'd be crazy not to take it," Clara agreed, reaching for one of the glasses. "We've got no one else interested. But, at the same time, we need to play hardball too. We deserve a good contract. Let's make sure we remember that."

"Hardball," Maisie said with a firm nod. "On it." She took a huge sip of her drink, her eyes fluttering shut.

Clara laughed softly, which admittedly, felt good. Maisie wouldn't know how to play hardball if she tried. She was too...*free.* "You can leave this part to me. I'm good at negotiating."

"You are," Amelia said, licking the salt off her lips. "And we appreciate everything you're doing for us and the company."

"Thanks," Clara said before taking a sip of her drink. The tequila hit first followed by the citrus sourness of the lime and then the sharpness of the salt.

She followed it up with another sip when Maisie asked, "Now let's talk about Sullivan."

"There's nothing to talk about," Clara insisted, setting her glass back down on the table.

"Sure, there is," Maisie said with a sly smile. "Like how good he looks?"

Mouthwateringly delectable. "He doesn't look terrible," Clara conceded.

Amelia asked, "Was it weird, seeing him again? You must have felt something. It's been so long."

I felt everything. The guilt of keeping a big secret. The heartbreak of knowing the man she once loved no longer existed and had walked out on her. The yearning to run into his arms and stay there because it had once felt so good. The anger and desire to punch him in his handsome face. Feeling like it was impossible to explain all that, she shrugged. "I feel confused. I feel like I owe him the truth. I feel like Mason is owed a father. I feel like I wish things were different. That Sullivan was different. I wish he would have answered the damn phone when I called, instead of the woman. I wish he would have called back."

Amelia frowned. "That's a lot of wishes."

"It is," Clara agreed then took another long sip, adding moisture to her dry throat. She'd rarely talked about Sullivan to her sisters, particularly about Sullivan being Mason's father. She'd swallowed and forged on, doing what had to be done. "But as much as I wish everything were different, I can't undo the past."

"You're right, you can't," Maisie said.

And the past wasn't pretty. When he was six years old, Sullivan's mother received her breast cancer diagnosis. She went through repeated treatments for ten years. She fought so hard, but ultimately, the cancer took her. In the wake of losing his wife, Sullivan's father became a drunk, and soon after, an angry drunk. He'd turned abusive and took his rage out on Sullivan.

"Well," Amelia said with a shrug. "If you ask me, you shouldn't have to undo the past. Sullivan left and completely ignored his life here. You were left to pick up the pieces after. You don't owe him shit as far as I'm concerned."

This all seemed like a nightmare she couldn't wake up from. "I never thought he'd come back."

Maisie slid her finger against the rim of her margarita glass, gathering up the salt. "You're not alone. Even Hayes said he was shocked to find out Sullivan was back in town."

"Which begs the question, why is he here?" Clara asked.

"Who cares?" Amelia shot back. "I think Sullivan has done enough damage already. Let's just hope he realizes no one wants him here and then he'll quickly go back to where he came from."

Clara nodded.

Maisie licked the salt off her finger and offered, "I say just ride out his time here. Keep Mason close and out of his sight. You need to do what's right for Mason, and until you know Sullivan is mentally stable, as far as I'm concerned, it's your right as his mother to protect him."

Clara didn't even want to voice the thought, but couldn't stop herself. "But what if he *is* mentally stable? What do I do then? Tell him he has a kid I never told him about?

Where would we even go from there? What would that look like for Mason?" Her head *hurt*. Her heart too. Sullivan was never supposed to come home. He didn't even come home for his father's funeral after he passed away a few months back. This wasn't the plan. This had never been the plan. She rubbed her throbbing temples. "I can't process how to deal with all this. Sullivan has a history of loving and leaving in a very cruel way. I won't let him do that to Mason. I can't."

Silence settled in, until Maisie asked, "So what are you going to do, then?"

"Protect Mason, no matter what."

Of course, her sisters didn't miss that she hadn't totally said her piece yet. "And?" they asked in unison.

"And Maisie's right," Clara continued, spinning her margarita glass between her fingers. "I need to see exactly the type of man Sullivan Keene is now. If he's worthy, if it's in Mason's best interest, then I'll tell him the truth and face the fallout."

Amelia looked skeptical. "You're really going to be able to do that?"

"Yes," Clara said with total certainty. "I have no other choice. If he'd stayed in Boston and forgot all about us and River Rock, I wouldn't tell him. Not ever. But for some unknown reason, he's back. He's spending his suspension *here*. I think it's important to find out why. Not only for Sullivan, but for Mason too."

Heavy silence descended around the kitchen table full of half-empty margarita glasses.

"I really hate to be the one to point this out," Maisie said, hesitantly, "but you did love him once. What if this gets, I don't know...messy?"

"It won't get messy," Clara promised, mostly to herself.

"It can't, not with Mason in the center of it all. Besides, things are different now."

"Why?" Amelia asked.

"Because this guy isn't *my* Sullivan. He's not the guy I loved. And this guy he is now, the one splashed all over the tabloids and fighting in bars, is not a man I could ever love."

Just after seven o'clock in the evening, Sullivan finished tying up the shoelaces of his boots before leaving his apartment. It was built above a barn, and the floors creaked beneath his weight. He'd rented for the month from old man Bart, an eighty-year-old local. Luckily for Sullivan, Bart, who rented his apartment to help pay his bills, was between tenants. The apartment was a far cry from Sullivan's upscale and modern condominium in Boston, but the rustic nature reminded him of when he used to work on a cattle ranch in his youth, during the summers.

A double bed rested against the far wall with a red-and-black quilt on top of dark gray sheets, all things Sullivan had bought upon arrival. A small galley kitchen with a tiny stove occupied the space beside a sink and a fridge. A mix of oak and dust lingered in the air, but somehow, the smell suited the place. Despite all the pleasing decorations, Sullivan felt restless, so he grabbed his keys off the small table next to the door then headed outside, leaving it unlocked behind him. He had nothing worth stealing other than his clothes. When he trotted down the rickety wooden steps, they groaned beneath him. It came as no surprise to see his landlord sitting on his porch in his old rocking chair, smoking a cigarette. "How are you today, Bart?" Sullivan called.

"Just fine. The sun will set tonight and rise tomorrow,"

the old man said with a smile that was missing a couple of teeth.

Bart's life was simple, and that suited him. If Sullivan was being honest, he envied that about him. If all Sullivan had to worry about was the sun rising and setting, life would be easy. "Enjoy the rest of your night."

Bart waved him off and took another sip from his coffee cup before puffing on his cigarette.

Sullivan was on the road soon after. River Rock's streets were never busy, especially compared to the streets of Boston. It had taken some time getting used to a big city. Sure, Sullivan had spent a lot of time in Denver while in college, but Boston felt like a world away from River Rock. The people were different, the smells, the scenery. Nothing felt the same, and for a long time, Sullivan had preferred that.

When he finally reached River Rock's downtown, he pulled over at the curb in front of a 2-hour parking sign and got out. Downtown River Rock held none of the riches of a big city, but it doubled in charm. Quaint brick storefronts hugged the street. Owners decorated their shop's doors, drawing in the visitors who came for the views of the Colorado mountains, the western country life, and the quiet countryside. All the things Sullivan had been more than happy to leave behind in his early twenties.

Now, as he crossed the road, he felt more at home than he ever did in Boston, but it surprised him how much had changed here. Not the familiar scents of a mix between fresh-cut flowers and sunshine, but the modernized stores. Long gone were all the old shops Sullivan remembered. He came to a stop outside River Rock's police station. Years back, the police had taken ownership of the old courthouse on Main Street with its big white columns in front. Inside the station, the space had been modernized, with the reception desk at the front, near the waiting room, where he found the receptionist, Phillis, working. She had black-dyed hair, a face full of wrinkles, and bright nail polish and lipstick.

She whistled, setting her phone back on the receiver. "My word, Sullivan Keene. It's been a long time since you've been home."

She'd worked there for as long as Sullivan could remember and was well past retirement age. He smiled at her. "It's been far too long."

"Indeed," Phillis said. "What can I do for you today?"

"Is the chief in?"

"He is," Phillis reported. "Here, I'll buzz you in. Go on back and see him. He's in the same office."

Seven years ago, Sullivan had spent a lot of time at the station. Not from getting in trouble. John Taylor, the chief of police, had taken him in at sixteen when Ronnie had declined to step up as Sullivan's guardian due to his busy work schedule. Sullivan had lived with John until he headed off for college.

On his way down the hallway, Sullivan waved to a few cops looking his way. He finally stopped outside the corner office. "Still working too late, I see," he said by way of greeting.

The chief's head snapped up. "Well, well, so the gossip around town is actually right this time. You're back?"

Sullivan nodded. "I am. Just for a month."

John rose and came around the desk to give Sullivan a rough hug. "It's damn good to see you."

"You too," Sullivan said, stepping out of the embrace. John and Sullivan talked often, and he always came to Denver whenever Sullivan had a game. He'd always been more of an uncle to Sullivan than Ronnie had even been. Even more of a father figure than Kurtis. "Listen, I can't stay long. I'm meeting Hayes for drinks. Can we catch up over breakfast?" With the chief, it was always meeting over breakfast. His days were too busy for anything else.

John nodded. "There's a great little place a block down called The Kitchen. Shoot me your schedule, and we'll fit it in."

"Will do." Sullivan moved to the door then glanced back. "You know it's a little after seven o'clock, right?"

The chief swatted at the air. "Work is work. Enjoy those drinks, Sullivan."

Thoroughly dismissed, Sullivan shook his head with a laugh then headed back outside. He headed back down Main Street until he slowed in front of the bar with the KINKY SPURS signage. Suddenly, A kid ran toward him.

"Sully. Sully. Can I get an autograph?"

He'd never liked the nickname the media gave him, but felt rude correcting anyone who used it. "Hey, now, that would be my pleasure." He accepted the pen and a notepad and went down to one knee. "What's your name?"

"Dakota," the kid said, beaming.

When he scribbled his signature, he took a guess and asked, "You look like you've got strong arms. Do you play baseball?"

Dakota's grin widened. He gave a fierce nod. "I'm a pitcher too."

Sullivan handed over the notebook along with the pen. "Keep at it, kid. You'll be in the major leagues before you know it."

"Yeah?" The kid's eyes sparkled.

"Oh, yeah," Sullivan said, rising. "All it takes is hard

work and practice." He smiled at the kid and then at his mother, who had joined them.

"Thank you so much," she said, her hand pressed to her chest. "He's such a fan of yours."

Sullivan felt a world of guilt fall on his shoulders. He forced another smile before walking away. The last thing he should be to anyone was a role model. He entered the bar, finding a classic country western décor, only this one felt like the real deal, unlike the ones he'd seen on the East Coast. Wood paneling covered the walls, and tables were spread out between two stages, one holding the band's equipment and the other supporting a mechanical bull. By that bull, he spotted his buddies, Hayes Taylor and Beckett Stone, sitting at a table with beers in front of them. Beckett was Hayes' closest friend, and even though they were three years older, they'd welcomed Sullivan into their fold. He never forgot their kindness.

Before joining them, Sullivan said to the pretty brunette behind the bar with a name tag that read MEGAN, "I'll take a Foxy Diva, if you've got one." He remembered her from high school, but she'd never run in his circle of friends.

"Coming right up," she said, turning away to fetch his drink.

When Sullivan headed for the table, he caught the attention of his friends. Both Hayes and Beckett had matching grins on their faces.

"Sully. Sully. Can I get your autograph?" Hayes smirked, waving his napkin.

Sullivan snorted. "I'd make you pay for an autograph." A burst of laughter was followed by rough, manly hugs. When Sullivan took a seat next to Hayes, he said, "It's good to see you both."

Hayes twirled his beer bottle between his fingers. "We wondered when you were going to come for a visit."

Sullivan felt shame roll over him. These men had been at his side when his father turned into a man Sullivan didn't recognize. A man full of hatred and rage. "I should have come home sooner."

"Seven years sooner," Beckett remarked.

Sullivan let the dig go. He deserved that. He'd kept in touch over text and the odd phone call, but it wasn't enough. "Yeah, man, definitely should have." He glanced at Hayes. "I'm sorry I wasn't here for Laurel's funeral. There's no excuse. I should have been here." Hayes had lost his wife, and Sullivan still felt like an asshole for sending flowers instead of coming to her funeral. But he'd been a selfish prick, and only thought of how coming home would affect him.

Hayes cupped Sullivan's shoulder, only warm affection on his face. "We all get why coming back here was hard for you. No one faults you for staying away."

Yeah, because at that time, his father was still alive. Sullivan had been unable to face him. Hell, he wasn't sure he could face him now if he were still alive.

Breaking into Sullivan's thoughts, the bartender set his beer in front of him and gave the group a smile. "Let me know if you want seconds or some grub."

"Thanks, Megan," said Beckett. After she walked away from the table, he added, "That's Nash Blackshaw's wife."

"You don't say?" The Blackshaw name was a big one in River Rock, due to their cattle company—the very one Sullivan used to work at during his teenage summers—and Nash was the youngest Blackshaw brother. "I heard from Ronnie that they opened a dude ranch at the farm."

Beckett nodded. "Yeah, they ran into some financial

trouble when Mr. Blackshaw passed away, but the farm and ranch are strong."

"Are you still working for them?" Sullivan asked then took a sip of his beer. Foxy Diva was crisp and fresh, reminding him a little of Clara.

Beckett shook his head. "I'm working for Nash now. We train and sell horses. He's got a good thing going there."

Sullivan swung his head toward Hayes, who smiled. "I help out when I can. You know how I love breaking horses with bad attitudes, but I'm back on the force now."

News to Sullivan. He never knew Hayes had *left* his job as a cop. "You quit the force?"

Hayes looked like he had a story to tell, but he smiled it away. "Took a break for a while, but law enforcement is where I should be."

Sullivan nodded and took a long chug of his beer. Hayes had been bred into law enforcement and came from a long line of good men and women who'd served the community of River Rock.

When he lowered his bottle to the table, Beckett leaned back in his seat and said, "All right, buddy, the chitchat is great, and I'm damn glad to see you, but fill in the missing pieces. You could have gone anywhere to serve out your suspension or stayed with the team. Why come back to the one place you said you'd never return to?"

Sullivan's throat began to tighten, but he swallowed past his issues with sharing. He'd come home to make things right, no matter how uncomfortable it made him. "Things, after my mom died, have been rough. This last recent bar fight was enough of a wake-up call that I needed to get my head on straight, and now that my father is dead, I needed to come home to deal with the shit I've been running from." Being back in River Rock wasn't easy. It was hell. Everything in here reminded him of his sweet mother, dead in the cold ground, and the cruel father who used his fists more than his words.

"It's good, you know, dealing with it all," Beckett said with a firm nod.

Hayes nodded as well. "All that shit, back then, was a lot for you to take on." He cupped his shoulder. "It's good you came back. About time to heal those wounds."

Sullivan figured that was about as much as they were going to talk about feelings and such since Beckett changed the subject. "I heard today you went out to the Carters' place." A little smirk lifted the corner of his mouth. "How did that go?"

"I'm not exactly sure," Sullivan commented.

Hayes' eyebrow lifted. "You're not dead or marked up at all, so I'd say it went well if those Carter sisters didn't kill you."

"Good point," Sullivan hedged.

Beckett asked, "What was it like, seeing Clara again?"

"Weird," Sullivan admitted. He took another long sip of his drink before he continued, "It's like I know her, but I don't."

Obviously, this was common knowledge, since Beckett agreed with a nod. "She's changed a lot in the last seven years."

"She had to," Hayes interjected. "A kid will do that to anyone."

Sullivan felt the blood leave his face. Admittedly, he'd hoped he'd come back to River Rock and discover that Clara had found someone better than him. He'd never had the balls to ask anyone if she had married. Only now, the thought twisted him up. "A kid?"

Hayes nodded. "His name is Mason. Good kid. She's a really great mom."

Sullivan bit back hot jealousy, well aware he had no right to be anything but happy for her. "Is she still together with the dad?"

The country music playing through the speakers seemed to fade away as Beckett shook his head. "She's also not married."

A million things crossed his mind, but only one thing stood out as most important. "Who's the dad?" Sullivan asked.

Hayes waited for a couple to pass by their table and take a seat, then he answered, "Since it's none of my business, I've never asked Clara or Maisie directly, but word around town is that she had a one-night stand and didn't know how to reach the father."

"That's a shame," Sullivan muttered. She deserved far better than that. "She's raised her son on her own, then?"

Hayes nodded, giving an affectionate smile. "Like I said, she's a very good mother."

Sullivan reached for his beer and took a long sip. He wondered what kind of mother she was. Sweet, stern, loving, fair? Deep down, he imagined she was probably a little of all that, just like Sullivan's mother had been. That kid was probably Clara's whole world. "How old is Mason?"

"Six," Beckett said and then shook his head, adamant, at whatever crossed Sullivan's face. "The kid isn't yours, buddy. We all know Clara. She's far too honest to ever lie about something so serious."

"True," Sullivan hedged. Though, something stirred in his chest, something edgy and wary. Because Sullivan did know Clara, and he knew for sure she'd most certainly lie to protect someone she loved.

4

Clara woke up fighting a headache from last night's margaritas and the million thoughts that kept her tossing and turning all night. How could she keep Mason in his safe little bubble? She'd was locked away in her home office that had once been the dining room. Her antique wooden desk had a comfortable chair behind it, and an old refurbished buffet on the far wall held all her files. She'd gone to college for business, and owning a successful brewery had always been the end goal. Only, she'd never expected the process to be so tedious and repetitive. "I appreciate you sending the offer over, Ronnie," Clara said into her phone tucked between her ear and shoulder. She'd had this same phone call three other times today.

"But you're not happy with our terms?" Ronnie asked, his voice far past patient.

"Whether I'm happy or not isn't the problem," Clara countered. "This morning, a couple other offers came in from two other distributors." They'd arrived with very little warning. Apparently, Three Chicks Brewery was hotter than any of them had imagined. Maisie was the reason, Clara didn't doubt that. Her sister had taken their little brewery to the next level by holding a festival on the premises that blew them out of the park. Now it was Clara's turn to push the brewery even further. "I'll need to review these offers with my sisters before we make a final decision," she told Ronnie. "I'll be in touch once we do."

A long pause. "That's fine, Clara. Talk soon."

She ended the call, returning her phone to the receiver, and faced the contracts on her desk. The process of signing with a distributor was far more complicated than she'd originally thought. Every offer was different, from the pricing of the product, to their advertising and promotion budgets and plans, to shipping costs, to incentive programs, to how the distributor planned to sell the brand. But her biggest problem today?

Sullivan. And all the things her heart felt with his return home.

She turned in her swivel chair and looked out the window to the big oak tree outside, its branches dancing in the slight breeze. Part of her, hated him with a blinding rage for offering her the world and then taking it away in the blink of an eye. The other part of her, missed his love. There had never been anyone after Sullivan; no one who could compare. Remembering that wonderful side of him, her mind slowly left the room, taking her back to what felt like another life entirely.

"Don't look at me like that, Clara," said Sullivan, *hovering over her while she lay on a blanket.*

"What way, Sullivan?" She smiled.

He shook his head, grinning back. "Goddamn it, girl, you know what you're doing. When you look at me like that, you know I'll give you anything and everything you want, don't you?"

She laughed and cupped his face. "Goddamn it, boy, you know I only want you, don't you?"

"Damn straight." He smirked, full of manly pride, then his mouth dropped to hers.

The kiss was sweet and soft and teasing and all but melted her bones. She'd kissed a few boys, but none like Sullivan Keene. None who meant it like him. Almost like he needed to touch her, hold her, to make his world right.

After he gave a low groan, he backed away and shifted onto his side, resting his head on his hand. "Better stop that, or your Pops is going to bury me six feet under."

Clara mirrored his posture. "We both know who would win in a fight, and it wouldn't be my Pops."

Sullivan laughed and winked. "Well, in that case..." He wrapped his arm around her, tugging her in close. She stared up at him, her heart breaking for the pain she could see hidden behind the strong wall he projected. His mother had died two years ago after a long, cruel fight with cancer. But nothing got better after her death; it only got worse.

Her heart bled for him. "Everything's going to be all right, Sullivan. You'll see."

His brows drew together as emotion filled those breathtaking eyes. "I know it will. Because one day we'll get married and I'll give you the life you've always wanted. Make you the happiest girl in the world."

"I already am the happiest girl," she said.

The heartbreak faded with his warm smile. "Yeah, but you'd also really like the wedding and the dress and all that girly shit."

"You're right," she said, lifting up her head until she brought her mouth close to his. "I would like all that girly shit."

This time, she kissed him, and she wouldn't let him pull away when he groaned again.

A car door slamming brought Clara's attention back to

the work in front of her. She blinked, surprised to find tears on her face. Before Sullivan's mother died, everything had been easy between them, simpler, with a whole world ahead of them. Back then, Sullivan was different. She'd been different. More carefree and not so guarded. She missed that old version of herself.

Her office door burst open. She was unsurprised when Amelia and Maisie strode in. She'd called them a half hour ago. "I've got good news and bad," she announced, getting right to the point of the meeting. "What do you want first?"

"The good," said Maisie, taking a seat on the tufted chair in the corner by the window.

Amelia sat on the armrest. "Yup, always the good first."

Clara took a big, deep breath, steadying herself before addressing them again. "This morning, two other distributors reached out with offers to represent us."

"No shit?" Amelia asked, eyes huge.

Clara nodded. "True."

"Wow," Maisie said with a bright smile. "That is amazing news."

"It's the exact news we've been waiting for," Clara agreed. "But that said, the terms are terrible."

Maisie's smile fell. "That's the bad news, then?"

"Exactly," Clara confirmed. She pushed away from her desk and rubbed her eyes, careful not to smudge her mascara. "Ronnie sent over his terms too." When she dropped her hands, she glanced between her sisters and added, "All of the contracts definitely benefit the distributors more than us and give them far more control than I'd like."

"We definitely don't want that," Amelia said. "This is our company. Our beer. Pops' beer."

"Hell yeah," Maisie agreed. "What can we do now?"

"It's simple," Clara explained, rising and moving to the window, looking out at that big tree again. "We need leverage to lessen their profit margin. All three companies have offered us a 28 percent profit margin for the distributors' share, which would give us seventy-two percent of the profit. We need to get that number closer to twenty-five or less so we end up with seventy-five percent of the profit."

From behind Clara, Maisie asked, "Okay, ignoring profit margins, do any of the distributors stand out?"

Clara turned back around. "Ronnie's looking like our best shot. His company knows how to sell craft beer. They made Moose Ridge huge in a very short time. They've got everything we need, including a brand manager responsible for Foxy Diva's product line. Most importantly, they're financially strong and growing."

"But the profit margin?" Amelia asked.

"But the profit margin is a problem," Clara agreed, moving around to sit on the edge of her desk. She folded her arms and told it to her sisters straight. "I don't want to rush this and accept whatever deal they throw at us. We need a better offer, but we need leverage to ask for a better one."

Maisie nibbled her lip then asked, "All right, how do we do that?"

"And there lies the problem," Clara said, dead serious. "Do either of you have any ideas?"

"Oh, this is bad," Amelia said, the color draining from her face. "You *always* have ideas."

"Don't faint on me," Clara said with a soft laugh. "We've got this. Something will come to me. It always does. We just need to think bigger. We need more buzz, more exposure, more reasons that will have these distributors fighting over us. The offers all expire in a month, so we've got time to turn this around in our favor."

"Oh, that's good," Maisie said.

Clara agreed with a nod as the alarm on her cell phone beeped. She headed back around her desk and turned it off. "I need to grab Mason from school, but let's think on this. We need to push ahead. We need to make this work for all of us." Even if Maisie agreed to a lesser share of profit now that she only did graphic design for the company, they all needed this company to succeed. "This is it, our one chance to take our little company and make it big." She moved to the door and looked back at her sisters. "Until we get what we want, we can't stop. Got it?"

"Got it," her sisters said in unison.

Clara took a step out the door when Maisie added, "But you're going to think of something, right? I mean, this is your wheelhouse Clara, not ours."

Clara smiled back at her. "I'll come up with something brilliant. I promise."

Late into the morning, Sullivan arrived at the office of Dr. Elizabeth Stevens. Determined to deal with his past and be a better man by the time he left River Rock and to leave all his trauma there, behind him, he figured a therapist was his best way forward. The office was located in an old Victorian home a block off Main Street. He climbed the porch steps, opened the front door, and was greeted by a surprise. Working behind the desk was Gloria Winters, the mother of a player from his old baseball team.

"Sullivan Keene, as I live and breathe," she said, her wise brown eyes just as he remembered them. "My goodness, it's so nice to see you."

Sullivan shut the door behind him. "You as well, Mrs. Winters. How's Kenny doing?"

She grabbed a picture off her desk, flipped it around, and showed him Kenny with his wife and three young children. "He's a busy family man now, not playing much baseball these days. But he's got my oldest grandson playing local tee-ball."

"Good stuff," Sullivan said.

Before he could even sit down, the door next to Mrs. Winters' desk opened. Dr. Elizabeth Stevens was younger than he was expecting, but still older than him. He guessed mid-to-late forties, with shoulder-length brown hair that was lighter on the ends and hazel eyes that seemed far too clever for her years. "Mr. Keene, please come on in." Elizabeth moved aside for Sullivan to enter the room consisting of a large desk with a computer and telephone, along with a seating area.

Sullivan waited for her to close the door, feeling ready to climb out of his skin. "Listen, Doc, I'm new to all this."

"That's all right," Elizabeth said with a gentle smile, moving to the far seat next to the beige leather sofa. She picked up her notepad and then kindly but firmly pointed to the couch. "Please take a seat, Mr. Keene. I'm here to listen. It's really as simple as that."

He took his seat, forcing himself not to fidget as they shared quick niceties. Then a beat passed. Her stare was patient and calm and intrusive. They stayed that way for a good minute until the silence became dauntingly heavy. "I have no idea where to start," he admitted.

Elizabeth's trusting eyes warmed. "Why don't you tell me about why you decided to move away from River Rock?"

Sullivan considered her carefully, even if everything told him to look away. Small towns had a way of spreading gossip at hyper speed. A few talks with the local mothers around town, and Elizabeth had likely heard his history. He just hoped she had a code of conduct and didn't talk about her clients. "You haven't already heard about me?"

She held his gaze. "The story from your mouth is the only one I care about."

Her answer gave immediate comfort, and he felt his muscles slowly relax. "Why do you want to know about why I decided to move away?" he asked, honestly curious.

No emotion showed on her face. "I figured it's a good place to start, but feel free to begin wherever you feel more comfortable."

Either her intuition was spot on, or his former concern about gossip was true. He drew in a deep breath, wondering what would be an easier place to start. As he glanced to the window behind her desk, his mind drifted to a long-ago memory.

The sun was just beginning to set as Sullivan walked toward his house. He left his bicycle in the front yard long-past needing mowing. Two days ago, he'd turned twenty-one, and on his birthday, a day after graduating from the University of Denver on a full baseball scholarship, a scout had approached him. He hadn't been home for years now, staying with the local police chief and his son, Hayes, but he figured the news needed to be shared in person. Part of him hoped the good news would bring back a glimpse of the father Sullivan had once loved, the man who'd been at every game, cheering him on.

The house his mother had once loved was unrecognizable now. Her beloved gardens were dead, weeds overrunning everything. He headed up the porch steps and knocked on the door. "Dad?" he called.

A loud bang followed by a few more echoed in the house before the door whisked open. His father stumbled into the door-

way, and Sullivan had to brace himself against the shock. He barely recognized this man. His father had to have lost fifty pounds, and his face was sunken in and hollow. He smelled like rotten tequila and had dirt covering his hands and face. His brown hair was greasy and long, and his once-brown eyes now looked nearly gray and lost. So damn lost. A quick look inside the house, and Sullivan spotted glass on the floor, the smashed family pictures in the hallway.

"Why don't you fucking listen?" his father roared, snapping Sullivan's gaze up. "I told you to stop coming here. You're not fucking welcome." Spittle formed at the corners of his mouth.

Sullivan knew why. He took after his mother's side of the family, and he suspected when his father looked at him, he saw a painful reminder of all he'd lost. "I've got some good news—"

"Get off my property."

Sullivan took a step forward. "Dad, I—"

"You never fucking listen."

His father lunged then, and completely caught off guard, Sullivan took a direct punch right under his eye. He went soaring back to land on the grass below the porch steps, feeling the blood flowing down his face.

"Was that the first time your father hit you?"

Sullivan blinked, yanking himself out of that dark time in his life. He didn't realize he'd spoken the story out loud. He rubbed his arms, trying to fight the chill. "No, but it was the last."

Elizabeth gave a soft, sympathetic smile.

He forced himself to continue, and it all flowed easily. They talked more about that day, about his mother's death, and more about the abusive man his father became. Each minute felt longer than the one before it, and when he finally got to leave, he'd nearly gulped at the air outside.

As he walked to his car, his head started to pound, and

he kept thinking he should feel something, but all there was in his chest was emptiness. He'd left his truck parked at the curb and walked downtown. People were everywhere, shopping and enjoying the day, but Sullivan couldn't shake the haunting darkness shadowing him. He stopped at the local coffee shop; Hot Brew and Eats, the signage read. The shop definitely hadn't been there when Sullivan lived there. It used to be a breakfast hotspot, but they'd kept the old retro-style booths, refinishing the seats in brown leather instead of the red he remembered. He made it to the counter, where a young brunette stood wearing all black with a black apron. Her eyes went huge when she saw him, indicating she watched baseball.

"Hi!" she said, excitedly. "Um, what can I get you?"

"Coffee with cream," he said.

"Sure, coming right up." She blushed, then hurried to process his payment. As she did so, a couple of women entered the shop, behind him.

"We've got ten minutes before school is out."

"We'll make it," the other woman said. "Besides, I need caffeine if I'm going to get through the meeting with the principal."

"Girl, you've got this. Get your Mama Bear claws ready."

Sullivan smiled to himself at their conversation, and he glanced down at his watch. Three o'clock in the afternoon. He remembered when his mother watched over him like that, when she would meet him at the elementary school to walk him home, and sometimes have baked cookies waiting for him. He missed those moments with her.

"Here's your coffee."

Sullivan jerked his gaze up, finding the young woman offering him the paper cup. "Thanks."

She blushed again and held up her cell phone. "Can I

get a photo? No one will believe me when I tell them I met you."

"Yeah, let's do that," he said with a smile, angling his body to get closer to her over the counter.

After she snapped her photo, he said his goodbyes, smiled at the confused women who obviously wondered who he was, and left the coffee shop. He planned to go left and head back to his rented truck. Instead, his feet had him moving right while he sipped his coffee. He kept his eyes down, not wanting to make eye contact. Fame came with the job; he never minded it. Hell, he liked the kids. He just didn't think they should look up to him. Many of his teammates had it all together, wife, kids, the perfect modern-day family. Sullivan felt stuck in a Groundhog Day scenario where he carried on numbly, feeling nothing, until all of a sudden, he felt everything. It never ended well.

Eventually, he ended up at River Rock's Elementary School. The old schoolhouse with the large silver bell above the door had only a hundred or so students a year. Last night, Sullivan thought about packing his bags and getting far away from this town—from the nagging feeling that Clara's one-night stand story didn't add up. Even as he waited by the light post, sipping his coffee, he knew he should leave. What if her story seemed off because this kid was his? What was he going to do about it? Be a dad? The thought was damn near laughable. He was failing at keeping his own life together and his anger in check. But there he was, at the schoolhouse, waiting for...he wasn't quite sure.

People passed by him on the sidewalk, moms and dads picking up their laughing and smiling children. But when Sullivan spotted Clara parking and then exiting her prac-tical sedan, a car he couldn't even imagine her owning, his feet remained rooted to the spot. She'd always been responsible and had a good head on her shoulders, but she hadn't been uptight or practical. She moved closer to the school, a huge smile on her face, the noise of the children near deafening. Sullivan scanned over every little face until he stopped at one, and he felt the ground drop from under him. The boy had light brown hair, a shade Sullivan recognized because the same color was on his own head. He saw a blur of jeans and a red backpack as the boy ran into Clara's arms and she squeezed him tight.

Time slowed. Sullivan had seen that smile on her face before. She used to smile at him that way. But then she caught sight of him, and she straightened up, her pretty eyes instantly becoming guarded, her smile disappearing.

Walk away now. He repeated it in his mind again and again, but his feet decided otherwise. He took the final steps to reach Clara and Mason then went down to his knees, feeling like the air had been sucked right out of his chest.

Mason watched him closely then his eyes slowly widened. "Whoa, you're Sully." He blinked. "And look, our eyes are the same."

Sullivan breathed past the tightness invading his chest. Now closer, Sullivan swore he was looking into his mother's eyes. Same shape. Exact same color, a little lighter than his. "Yeah, little man, they sure are." He glanced up at the woman who owed him answers. One look at Clara's face was all Sullivan needed as she wrapped her arms around Mason, drawing him back into her safe hold. *Damn.* The world shook beneath him when he saw her expression. Something he'd never seen on her face when they were together. Distrust. Caution. Sullivan knew then. Clara perceived him as a threat to Mason.

Sullivan had failed at many things, but *this*, there was no failure worse than seeing Clara feeling like she needed to protect the kid—*his kid*—from him. Hot anger pulsed through his veins, and crippling shame coursed through him until he couldn't even identify how he felt about this. "Care to explain?" he asked, arching an eyebrow at her.

Clara sighed then kissed the top of Mason's head. "Come to the house tonight at seven thirty."

"Why not now?" Sullivan barely held onto his composure, rising again.

She rubbed her hand through Mason's hair, making him laugh. "Because this little guy needs dinner and a bath before bed."

Right. A routine. "All right, seven thirty it is."

Clara gave him a nod then turned to Mason and clearly forced a smile. "Say goodbye to Sullivan."

"Bye," he said and then whirled around, booking it to the car.

Clara followed like a bomb hadn't been dropped on Sullivan's life.

5

Most days, Clara knew exactly how her day would go from the moment she woke up to the moment she went to bed. She had a schedule. A plan. Life never really changed much. But all her years spent worrying were finally coming to a head, and her worst fears were coming true. Her structured life was about to be blown to pieces.... Because Sullivan *knew*. She had no idea how he found out, or if it was a coincidence that he was walking by the school. Truth was, it didn't matter how he knew, only that her secret had come out. Clara could only sit with bated breath, hoping—*praying*—that Mason stayed safe through all of this and that Sullivan wouldn't insert himself in their son's life only to vanish without a word. As she watched a freshly bathed Mason jump into his single bed with the quilt made of patchwork in his room with pictures of baseball players on the walls, the ground felt unstable beneath her feet.

When Mason settled his damp hair against the pillow, he asked, "Mommy, how do you know Sully?"

"His name is Sullivan," she said, pulling the blankets up to Mason's chest.

"Yeah, Sullian."

"It's Sulli-*v*-an, sweetie," Clara said with a laugh. "You're missing the 'v,' and he's mommy's old friend."

"So cool." Mason watched Clara with his sweet, curious eyes, his brow slightly furrowed. "Does he make you sad?"

"Sad?" she asked, aghast. "Gosh, no. Why would you think that?"

Mason didn't skip a beat. "Because you looked sad when we saw him."

Kids really missed nothing. Ever. Though this was her problem to worry about, not his. She leaned down and pressed a quick kiss on his nose. "Mommy is fine, sweetie. You don't need to worry about anything. Okay?"

"Okay," Mason said. Then his eyes suddenly lightened. "Maybe one day he can play baseball with me."

"Maybe one day." Clara's heart took a direct hit at the images that appeared in her mind. At the happiness she could imagine and had once wished so damn hard for. Over the years, she'd wanted to find Mason a father, a good man to help raise him. But that wasn't real life, and no one had ever measured up. She tucked the sides of the blanket in tightly around Mason as she said, "Snug as a bug in a rug." She pressed another kiss to his forehead. "Love you, buddy."

"Love you, Mama."

With her heart lodged in her throat, she flicked off the light on her way out, leaving the door ajar to allow in a little light to chase the monsters away. Since hiding in her room and pretending this wasn't happening wasn't feasible, she headed down the hallway lined with photographs of the happy childhood she'd had with her sisters in spite of losing their parents

when they were young. That loss had taught Clara the impor-
tance of a life well loved and that happiness and love could be
born out of the darkest of places. She missed her parents, but
her grandparents' love had healed their absence. When she
finally reached the top of the staircase, she stopped at the sound
of Sullivan's laughter as Amelia and Maisie entertained him.
And that low rumble brushed over her senses, taking her back.

*The crowd's loud cheering vibrated against the metal baseball
bleachers as Clara clapped at the final strikeout that Sullivan
delivered to win the game. Fans cheered his name. The players
swarmed Sullivan, the elation of a winning season overwhelming
them. But then, Sullivan emerged from the players, his gaze not
for them, but for Clara. He took off his baseball hat and wiped the
sweat off his forehead with his arm as he jogged her way. She
hopped off the bleachers and met him at the short chain-link
fence.*

"Congratulations," she said then gave him a quick kiss.

He smiled when she backed away. "It's you, you know."

*"What's me?" she asked, sliding her arms around his sweaty
neck.*

*"The reason I'm so damn good at this." He winked. "You're my
good-luck charm."*

*"Oh, please," she countered with a snort. "This was all you.
Your talent. Your skill."*

*The crowd still cheered as he pressed a soft kiss on her cheek
then said in her ear, "Why do you think I work so hard? I'm
trying to impress you." When he leaned away and she caught his
amused look, he asked, "Is it working?"*

*"Hmmm," she said, pretending to ponder. "It's safe to say that
tonight you're going way past third base and all the way home."*

*His head tipped back, and he barked a laugh. A laugh that
made everything better.*

But then the laughter was gone, and in its place came a

hard reality. Seven years, Clara had wondered and questioned if the hard choices she made to keep Mason from Sullivan were the right ones. She supposed it was time to find out if she'd been right. She headed down the staircase, finding Sullivan with her sisters in the living room that consisted of a wood-burning fireplace and a big bay window that brought in bright, natural light during the day.

From his spot on the floral sofa, he lifted an eyebrow. "All tucked in?"

She nodded. "He'll be out for the night." She noted the two shot glasses and a bottle of whiskey on the rectangular coffee table.

Amelia left the accent chair she'd been sitting in and picked up the glasses and bottle and handed them to Clara. "I'll keep an eye on Mason for you while you two talk."

"Thanks," Clara said, feeling the biggest lump of her life rising in her throat.

Maisie approached next, giving Clara a quick kiss. "Call me later if you need to."

"I will," Clara said. "Thanks." When her sisters left the room, and with booze in hand, Clara said to Sullivan, "I don't want Mason to hear us. Let's go out to the barn."

"All right." He rose, slipped back into his boots, and then followed her outside.

She quickly crossed the yard and entered the barn's double doors, turning on the lights as she went inside. After setting down the booze on the ground, she grabbed two wooden stools by the doors and set them next to each other. Halfway inside the brewery but still able to see the dark sky scattered with stars, she sat, and Sullivan joined her.

A beat passed before Sullivan glanced sidelong. "Did you always know he was mine?"

She drew in a huge breath and pushed past the lump in

her throat, acknowledging that hard question with a nod. "There's never been anyone else." Nothing long term anyway. A handful of one-night stands over the years when Clara had needed a reminder that she was still a living, breathing woman, but she'd always used protection. The last time with Sullivan, she hadn't. Not even knowing where to begin, she figured she'd start at the beginning. "I called to tell you about him, but it wasn't you who answered." It was his lover. "I stopped calling after that."

Another long, heavy pause, as he put the pieces together of that phone call. "That night you called, it was to tell me about him?"

She nodded. At that time, she thought they had everything. That he still loved her. Needed her. She'd been wrong.

Sullivan cursed softly, giving his head a slow shake.

She pushed on to get through this, staring down at the dark whiskey in the bottle. "I thought about calling back again, but—"

"It's good you didn't."

She jerked her head to him in surprise. "It's good I didn't?"

Sullivan wasn't looking at her; he stared out at the bright full moon. "Earlier today, when I saw him, I was so angry that you would keep this from me, keep *him* from me. Until I saw you pull him back to protect him." He visibly swallowed. Hard. "Seven years ago, I was a punk-ass kid who had no business being around any child." He ran a hand through his hair, tension tightening his eyes that looked so much older now, like he'd lived lifetimes already. "I would have destroyed him."

Like my father destroyed me echoed between them.

Clara processed. The tabloids had women draped off

Sullivan but no stories about a committed relationship. He had just received a suspension. Was he reckless? A wild disaster? A total hot mess? "Will you destroy him now?" she managed.

"No," Sullivan said. Then he turned his head, holding her gaze. "But I'm aware I have to earn your trust for you to believe that."

She wasn't going to sugarcoat any of this. "You will because I don't trust you, Sullivan, not within an inch of my life. And I won't let you come into his life, mess it up, and then vanish." Because that's what he did. He left with no explanation. No care at all that he'd shattered her heart.

He gave a soft nod of agreement. "You're protecting him from me. I get it, Clara."

She hesitated, surprised by his response, when something dawned on her. In all her worries, she'd never imagined this version of history. But she saw now, plain as day, that Sullivan viewed this situation as a mirror of what he'd been through. That, on some level, he was just like his father. Her heart completely broke to pieces, regardless of their past. She remembered the bruises, the stitches, the pain, and the horror in his eyes. No matter what he'd done to her, the pain he caused, he wasn't an abuser. "I don't need to protect him from you physically—that's not what I'm saying here. Please tell me you know that."

He turned and gave a sad smile. "I know that."

He didn't believe her, but she needed him to. This time, she'd get her voice out and be heard, unlike last time when he stole that choice from her. "Please listen to me. You being like your father is *not* the reason I didn't tell you. Back then, I was terrified that you no longer wanted me, or anything to do with this town, and you wouldn't be interested in a child. I was never worried that you would physically hurt Mason or me. I was only worried you'd promise him the world then leave him, and if I'm honest, I'm still very, *very* worried that's exactly what you'll do."

"You've got a right to be worried about that." Torment and nameless things passed over his expression as he blew out a long breath and then ran his hands over his face. "Which is why you're in control here, not me. So, tell me: where do we go from here? Do we tell him? Do we leave this alone? What is best for him?"

"I don't know," she answered after a long moment. "This is all new territory for me. To be perfectly honest, I never thought you'd come back. I never thought we'd see you again. You were living out your dreams in Boston." She paused, considering then deciding on a way forward. "I'm only, and always, thinking of Mason's best interests, and if you want to be in his life in a positive way, I'd never stand in the way of that, but that's where the line is drawn."

He processed then nodded. "I understand."

"There's no reason to rush this," she continued. "You've got a month here. Let's just take it one day at a time. Meet Mason in a casual way. Get to know him. And then you can decide if you truly want a son and all the responsibilities that come with it." Scared to death of the future and Mason's well-being, she reached for his arm, feeling him jerk in surprise at her touch, but held firm. "Mason is thriving. He's happy. Let's keep that our only focus here."

"That's fair." Sullivan drew in a deep breath and stared down at her hand on his arm, warmth touching his features.

The touch felt too familiar, too warm. She quickly pulled her hand away and continued, "This isn't about us and what happened in the past. This is only about Mason and what is good for him." She pushed all her motherly instincts out and added firmly, "Let me make this perfectly clear, Sullivan. If I think for a second that your involvement will hurt Mason, I'll get a court order and fight like hell to keep you out of his life."

"You won't have to," he eventually said. "I would never let it come to that."

Oddly, she believed him. She looked out at the moon, hoping that he had his shit together enough to do what was right for a child, not just because he selfishly wanted that child in his life.

"Clara," he said, so softly she looked back at him.

His gentle gaze held hers. "I have no idea if it will make any difference or if it only makes me look worse, but I want you to know, that woman who answered the phone that night, I wasn't with her. She was a teammate's wife. I asked her to answer the phone because I knew, after that, you'd stop calling."

Clara wasn't sure how she felt about his admission. Did it hurt more knowing that? Or did it hurt less? She exhaled slowly, immediately fighting back against the thoughts. No matter that her heart twisted, she couldn't let her feelings get wrapped up in all this. Mason needed her strong and at her best. "Well, it had the intended effect. I never called again."

Their gazes held. He finally looked away. "Yeah, I guess it did."

❧

Sullivan embraced the hot burn of the whiskey sliding down his throat after Clara poured them both a shot. *A son?* He worried about being a role model to kids he didn't know, but a son of his own? He knew the dangerous line he walked here, the damage that could be done. It had been done to him. And he was a twenty-eight-year-old man who still hadn't recovered from the trauma of his past. He felt sick. He had hoped that Clara would have moved on, found happiness, but he realized she couldn't have moved on, because she had Mason. And Sullivan's leaving had only made that harder for her. He had to make this right. "Can I explain why I left?" he asked her.

She shook her head, adamant. "You don't owe me an explanation."

"I do."

In the darkest parts of his heart, the memory of what he'd done insinuated itself until he couldn't push it away. And it was in that quiet moment, with her next to him, he let himself remember the day that had haunted him for seven years.

Sullivan shut his eyes against the bright florescent lighting in the hospital as the doctor finished the final stitch near Sullivan's eyebrow. His father had hit him before, but this time, the sucker punch had landed at just the right angle to cause damage.

"All right, we're all done here," Doctor Clay Booth said. He pushed away on his stool and set his suture tools back on the tray next to him.

Sullivan sat up, ready to down a few painkillers and get the hell out of there. "Thanks, doc."

Doctor Booth slid back over on his stool and set his warm stare on Sullivan. "The nurse told me what you said happened to you. How about you tell me the truth?"

Sullivan swallowed. Hard. "There's nothing more to tell."

The doc's brows rose. "You got into a brawl with a stranger?"

"That's right." That part wasn't a lie either. Sullivan had gotten into a fight at his game last night, only he hadn't been injured.

He shifted under the weight of the doctor's penetrating stare.

"Listen, son, I know times have been hard for you and your family," the doc said, gently. "But this path, it's not going to lead anywhere good. Silence is never going to help you. You might not want to talk now, but if you need to, I'm a call away."

Everyone knew his father was an abusive prick. He'd been taken out of his home and was living with the police chief for that very reason. But what was there to talk about? Shit happened. "Appreciate that, doc, but like I said, I'm fine."

Doctor Booth gave a final long look before he nodded and headed out the door.

Sullivan exhaled the breath he'd been holding and sank his fists into his eyes, taking care not to touch the stitches. Once, the Keene name had meant something in this town. Now Sullivan was just that kid whose mom had died of cancer and who now had a drunk for a father.

"Keene."

Sullivan lowered his hands to find the Boston Red Sox's scout, Noah Larson, standing in the doorway. He'd been following Sullivan's career through his college years at the University of Denver. The timing sucked, and Sullivan wasn't quite sure what would have happened if the scout hadn't shown up at his father's house for Sullivan to sign some documents. He had never officially changed his address and forgot to tell the scout the address of his dorm. He'd been the one to pull Sullivan's dad off him. Sullivan couldn't fight back. He wouldn't. His father was a broken shell of a person. Not a man, just a weak, pitiful human. "I'm sorry for what you walked in on today," Sullivan said.

"Don't apologize," Noah said, taking a seat on the bed, next to Sullivan. "No father should ever do what I saw your dad do to you." He took Sullivan's chin and turned it, getting a better look at the stitches. "You want an out? A way out of this small town? Promise me good pitching and hard work, and I'll make your dreams come true." He offered a pen and a piece of paper. "You've *got talent, kid. It's time you use it. Come with me to Boston. Let me get you in front of people that matter and show 'em the pitches that have been keeping me coming back to see you."*

A warm breeze brushing over Sullivan's face shook him out of the memory. "What you didn't know was that the night before I left, I'd gotten into a fight with a player from the opposing team after the game. Just push-and-shove shit, but I remember how I felt. The anger, the rage that filled me when I punched that guy until blood poured from his nose." He paused to collect himself then continued. "The following day, the day my dad punched me, I stared up at him and recognized that anger on his face, the feeling of it. That day I realized I'm capable of the same kind of rage." Feeling her stillness next to him, he glanced her way, finding her watching him closely. "You've got to understand, Clara, it scared me. Scared me enough to leave, knowing you deserved better. That rage would have only festered if I'd stayed in River Rock. It would have eventually touched you. Maybe not by my hand, but in some way, and I couldn't let that happen. So I left, and for a very long time, that anger stayed gone." Until his father died.

Clara's lips pursed before her expression softened a little. "It wasn't your choice to decide what is good for me or not. That wasn't your right; it was mine. You should have told me why you were leaving. What was going on in your head."

He considered that, and he knew she was right. But he'd been a ticking time bomb back then. All he knew was that he couldn't let his instability touch her. "Whether it was my decision to make or not make is irrelevant now. I made that decision, and there is no changing that," he eventually said.

She sighed heavily. "So, where are you going with all this?"

He set his shot glass back down and turned to face her. "I want you to know I'm not pissing around here. I'm not the guy who left you seven years ago, hiding from the past. I've come home to face the shit I couldn't face before. To right so many wrongs. Because when I got the call that my dad had died, in my head, I was fine. It resolved everything. The bastard was dead, and I could finally move on. But slowly, I began to drown. The game wasn't enough anymore. Nothing was enough. And then, I just snapped again...all that anger and rage came back."

"Which led to the suspension?"

"That's right." He stared at his greatest mistake. For seven years, Clara had been living the life Sullivan should have had with her, with his son. He should have made things easier, better. And he'd run from that life like it was poison to him. He didn't come back for his father's funeral when his kidneys finally gave out. He donated any of the money left in his father's estate. It all sat like a painful memory he didn't want to resurface. But none of that should have impacted Clara. Clara had only wanted love. Why couldn't he have given her that? "The reason I'm telling you all this is so you know I'm not here to mess up anyone's lives. I'm here to make amends." And to show her he was serious, he added, "I've enlisted the help of Dr. Elizabeth Stevens."

Her brows lifted. "You're going to therapy?"

He nodded, spotting the surprise in her eyes. At one time, he would have felt shame at admitting he needed help. He didn't have that left in him. Now all he had was a purpose to heal all his broken pieces. "I'm putting in the work and doing what I should have done seven years ago and dealing with the trauma."

For a split second, the cold Clara he didn't know at all vanished and the soft Clara he knew all too well appeared.

"No one deserves to struggle. It's good you're looking after your mental health, Sullivan."

He nodded and rose, shoving his hands in his pockets, staring down at her as the bright moon cast warm light over them. And with those sweet eyes on him, Sullivan was hit with something completely unexpected. He still loved her. Madly. Deeply. And, for him, it felt like no time had gone by at all when she looked at him like that. "One step at a time. Take this slow and get to know Mason. That's the plan going forward."

In an instant, the warmth was gone and a stranger was staring at him with distrusting eyes. "That's the plan," she agreed.

"All right," he said, reaching back into his pocket to grab his wallet. "I'm staying in old Bart's apartment for the month. Here's my number." He handed her a card. "You'll be in touch?"

"I will."

"Then, we'll talk soon. Sleep tight." He turned away and crossed over the gravel driveway to his rented truck, knowing full well his plan didn't stop there. He mentally added one more task onto the list of what he needed to achieve before he left River Rock—*earn Clara's forgiveness.*

6

The next morning, Clara peeked open an eye to find a bright, sunny day. She shifted onto her side in bed and stared out her bedroom window to the branches of the trees waving in the slight breeze. Last night filled her mind. Nothing was playing out like she'd intended. She had expected Sullivan to book it, not for him to own up to his past mistakes and try to better himself. A part of her heart finally healed at knowing why he left. In that same spot, there was sadness that Sullivan's trauma had made him believe he was better off gone. Alongside that, was cold hard rage that Sullivan's father had done this to him. That he'd taken a loving guy and destroyed him. That he stole away the Sullivan that Clara had blindly loved.

"Mama. Wake up." A blur of navy-blue pajamas with astronauts on them rushed into her room.

Her mattress bounced as Mason jumped on her bed a second later. "Morning, honey," she said, gathering him in her arms. He gave a boisterous laugh as she kissed his cheeks repeatedly. "Did you have good dreams?"

"No dreams." He looked at her with those sweet eyes. "Do I have to go to school today?"

"Yup." She gave him another big kiss while he wiggled out of her hold. "Go get dressed, and I'll make you some pancakes."

"Yum. Paaaaancakes."

As fast as he'd come into her bedroom, he was gone, having no idea his life might change forever any day now. *Be his shield.* Nothing could hurt Mason, not if she simply held strong. And while Sullivan seemed to want to make amends and do the right thing, she didn't know him anymore. *One step at a time,* she reminded herself. Determined to get her day started, she slid out of bed, aware of the slight headache that would most likely follow her for the rest of the day because of those shots.

While she got ready, tossing her hair up in a tight pony-tail and dressing in jeans and a blouse, she tried to find all the hatred she'd had for Sullivan. But by the time she headed down the stairs, she realized that anger had vanished after their talk last night. He'd been honest and open, and now she had the answers she'd always needed. It felt like an apology even if the words were never said directly.

The moment she entered the bright, sunny kitchen, Amelia handed her a coffee mug full of piping-hot coffee made just how Clara liked it. "Tell me everything," her sister stated. Amelia knew better than to ask Clara anything last night. She always needed time to gather her thoughts.

Clara chuckled then took a quick sip before setting it down to grab the frozen pancakes from the freezer as well as the sausages from the fridge. "We talked. That's what happened."

"Did it go okay?" Amelia asked, leaning forward, eyes bright with interest.

Only two years apart, Clara and Amelia were close. Maisie, being four years younger than Clara, had always been the *baby* sister, and only recently had their relationship blossomed into a friendship. Amelia was Clara's best friend. Back in the day, Clara's friends couldn't relate to a young single mom. They were off, busy with their lives, partying wildly, making plans for the future, while Clara had been changing diapers. Amelia had been there through the good, the bad, and the ugly. "He gave me the answers I needed, and promised to only do what's right for Mason. He said he's here to heal from his past, not to stir up trouble. We're going to take this day by day so he can get to know Mason before we make any big decisions." When Amelia's lips parted, Clara raised her hand. "Don't ask more than that. I'm still processing it all, so don't ask me how I feel about anything."

Amelia blinked. Twice. "I don't even know what to say."

Clara lifted a finger. "Is this wise, for him to see Mason?" Another finger lifted. "He's leaving in a month. What will happen after that?" She raised a third finger. "You two do have a lot of history together." And a fourth finger went up. "I'm happy for you, but worried because of Mason and because Sullivan really hurt you before."

"Yes," Amelia said with a firm nod. "All of that."

Clara understood her worry. Hell, she'd probably feel the same way in Amelia's shoes. She stuck the pancakes in the toaster then wrapped Amelia in a tight hug. "Thank you for worrying, but I'm okay. I'm not the girl he left behind. My head is right on my shoulders. Mason's well-being is all I'm thinking about right now."

Amelia stepped out of the embrace. "I guess that makes sense."

"Pancakes," Mason yelled, running for the table.

And just like that, the conversation was over and Clara turned on mom-mode. She got Mason to school on time and grabbed some wood-fired bagels at the bakery for the week ahead on the way home. By the time she got back to the brewery, the parking lot had a couple of extra vehicles and one white van as well as Maisie's car.

Clara parked in her usual spot near the house. She quickly took the bagels inside to the kitchen before heading to the barn. The moment she got close, she heard Sullivan's smooth voice. Another few steps, and she realized why—a news crew was interviewing him.

Maisie stood a few feet away, so Clara hurried to her side. "What is this?" she asked when she reached Maisie.

Her younger sister smirked. "All Sullivan's idea. He called Hayes late last night and asked if he could get a T-shirt and baseball hat with our logo on it. Then twenty minutes ago, Amelia called me and told me he'd shown up with reporters."

Clara followed Maisie's gaze to find Amelia talking to a male reporter, who stood next to Sullivan. Her breath quickened. He'd always looked good in worn blue jeans and a T-shirt, but the black T-shirt and baseball hat both had a THREE CHICKS BREWERY logo. He looked *hot* as he spoke to a female reporter and said into the microphone, "It's all very simple. I needed a break, and I'm taking that break at home. I have no intention of making the mistakes I've made in the past again. When my suspension is over, I'll be back and ready to play harder than ever."

"Anything you want to say to your fans?" the reporter asked.

Sullivan paused, his gaze meeting Clara's for a moment before he looked directly into the camera. "I'm sorry for my disappointing behavior. While I'm human and make mistakes, I'll do better going forward."

The interview ended with a few more questions, but Clara couldn't take her eyes off Sullivan. She didn't really know this *man.* Confident, determined, and centered—he'd been a twenty-one-year old kid when he left, and a total mess too.

Breaking into the silence, Maisie said, "All right, I've got to get to the studio, but see you tonight for dinner. Thank Sullivan for me. This was amazing exposure for us."

Clara still couldn't look away from Sullivan as his gaze fixed on her too. "Yeah, okay, bye," she said, without looking Maisie's way.

She swore she heard Maisie's laughter, but she couldn't tear her eyes away as Sullivan said his goodbyes to the news crew and made his way over. "What is happening?" she asked, trying to understand.

He lifted one shoulder. "My agent called and asked to set up an interview, since the press has been on me. I figured getting the brewery some free press would only benefit you. Have I overstepped?"

"Um, no," she said, finally finding her senses. "This was...Sullivan, you didn't have to do this for us."

He shoved his hands into his pockets, rocking back on his heels. "I know, but I wanted to."

"Well...thank you," she said, and the business part of her mind was smiling from ear to ear. Sullivan *was* famous. Companies paid him hundreds of thousands of dollars to wear their brands. And he'd done this for *free.* The extra exposure could also help her negotiate better contract terms with the distributors. "I mean it, thank you. You were right; this will definitely benefit us."

"Good." A warm, infectious smile crossed his face. "I'm happy to do it."

With the news crew packing up, Amelia approached. "Okay, that was just cool. Again, Sullivan, thank you."

"Anytime," he said as if this meant nothing. "Whatever I can do to help with this new venture, just ask."

Amelia gave Clara a quick look that she couldn't quite read before she addressed Sullivan again. "Listen, tonight we're grilling up some steaks for dinner. Hayes and Maisie are coming. Would you like to come too?"

His gaze swept to Clara, uncertainty in his expression.

Her mind stuttered for a moment. Every instinct inside her told her to say no. But, after what he'd done today and said last night, it was clear he was trying to do the right thing. And what better way to casually meet Mason than surrounded by all the people who loved him and would protect him as much as Clara would. "Yes, of course, you're more than welcome. Nothing better than saying thank you with a big steak."

"Okay, yeah," he said, but hesitation showed on his face.

Clara understood. "Bring a baseball glove, all right? Mason already told me he hoped you'd play some ball with him."

"All right." He gave a soft smile. "I'll bring a glove, then. What time?"

"Five thirty."

"I'll be here."

He exchanged a quick goodbye with Amelia and then was on his way back to his truck.

"Sorry if that's not what you wanted," Amelia said once

he was far enough away. "It just felt right after he did this for us today."

"It does feel right." Clara slid her arm through Amelia's. "They have to meet at some point. Might as well be with everyone who loves Mason."

Amelia chuckled. "So we can all kill him if he messes this up?"

"Precisely." Clara grinned, giving Sullivan a wave as he drove off.

&

Sullivan had faced down some of the best players in baseball. He'd gone up against the toughest reporters. But *this*... eyes the same color as his mother's watching him as he strode through the yard toward the picnic table, this was tougher. While Mason had Sullivan's mother's eyes, he could see Clara's cleverness in there too. Especially when Sullivan handed her a bouquet of daisies—her favorite flower—and a bottle of red wine. "Thanks again for the invite," he told her. His only plan earlier had been to begin to earn Clara's trust back and show her that his heart was in the right place. He didn't know how much he'd wanted the invite until they extended it. He was especially grateful when he saw Clara. She looked beautiful in the evening sun, but he suspected she'd prefer for him not to compliment her in front of Mason.

She sniffed the flowers then smiled. "Daisies. They're beautiful. Thank you." She gave Mason a quick look then gestured to the one person Sullivan didn't know. "This is Luka, Amelia's fiancé. Luka, this is Sullivan Keene." Tall and dark-haired, Luka stuck out among them as someone who didn't belong. He wore navy-blue slacks with a white dress shirt, making it obvious he worked in the city.

"Hey, man," Luka said, offering his hand.

Fiancé? Beckett had told him a while back that he and Amelia had broken up, but he'd never said a word about her becoming engaged. Sullivan returned a weak handshake. "Good to meet you."

"Likewise," Luka said then wrapped his arm back around Amelia.

It looked wrong. Sullivan only knew Beckett and Amelia together, but he forced himself to glance Clara's way as she asked, "Do you remember our cousin, Penelope?"

He smiled. "Yes, of course, it's nice to see you again, Penelope." Every summer, her big city parents sent her to River Rock to spend with her cousins. Only last time Sullivan saw her she'd been a kid.

Penelope waved. "Hey, Sullivan."

A beat passed. Clara finally took Mason by the shoulders. "Mason, you remember Sullivan, right?"

Mason nodded and took one look at Sullivan's baseball glove, then those bright eyes flicked up again. "I got a glove like that."

Sullivan released the breath caught in his throat. This, he could do, and do easily. "Why don't you go grab it and we'll throw some balls around?"

Mason's eyes went huge before he whirled to Clara. "Can I, Mama?"

"Just 'til dinner," she said, scuffing his hair.

She barely finished talking before Mason took off toward the shed. Clara laughed softly. "I think he secretly believes that playing ball with a professional baseball player makes him a professional too."

Sullivan chuckled. "Nothing wrong with believing that."

With Mason gone, the mood shifted and tension filled the air as Amelia and Maisie watched Sullivan closely. Penelope looked everywhere but at him. Everyone was on guard, waiting for him to fuck up.

Feeling like he was being squeezed from all directions, he rubbed the back of his neck, pushing past the churning in his stomach. "Listen, I get you're all worried. I told Clara last night, but I'll tell you now; I'm not trying to stir up trouble. I won't make a wrong move here. If this isn't a good thing, it ends. All right?"

Amelia's tight expression relaxed. She leaned into Luka's hold and replied, "All right."

Sullivan glanced at Maisie, who stared at him like she could read all his intentions on his face. "All good?"

She finally blinked and then gave a firm nod. "Keep to that promise, and we'll be fine."

"Good. We've cleared that up," Hayes said with a chipper voice. He gave Sullivan an approving hard slap on the back. "Now, let's just enjoy the rest of the sunlight we've got today."

And just like that, all the tension that lingered in the air vanished. Everyone went back to their conversations.

Clara moved closer to him, sniffing the flowers. "You remembered the daisies."

"Hard to forget. You did have them everywhere," he reminded her. She drew them on her binders, had stickers on her locker, and had them in jars all around her bedroom.

Before she could respond, Mason charged out of the shed, baseball glove in hand. "I'm ready!"

"Almost ready," Sullivan said when Mason reached them. He grabbed the Boston Red Sox baseball hat tucked into his back pocket that he'd picked up earlier in the day.

He sized it down then slid it onto Mason's head. "Now you're officially part of the Red Sox."

"Cool." Mason beamed.

Sullivan gave Clara a wink then headed off to the middle of the yard. He slid into his glove and turned around. "All right, buddy, show me how you throw."

Mason whipped the ball across the lawn, remarkably far, right into Sullivan's glove.

Impressed by the kid—*his* son—Sullivan jogged over to Mason. He caught Clara and her sisters watching them intently as he settled in front of Mason again. "Wiggle out your feet a bit." When Mason did as told, Sullivan added, "Yeah, that's better. Turn just a little," he instructed, gently adjusting Mason's body posture. "There it is. That's where you want your body to be. Don't forget to keep your eyes on me." Sullivan backed up a dozen steps then got into a catcher's position. "Hit me with it," he called.

And Mason did. Hard.

"How'd that feel?" Sullivan called, grabbing the ball from his glove.

Mason grinned from ear to ear. "That went fast."

"It did." Sullivan punched his glove then held it out. "Show me again."

Throw after throw, Mason got better and stronger, reminding Sullivan of himself as a kid. Time went by slowly, and Sullivan absorbed the conversation and laughter around him. The simple life. It felt familiar and yet a world away from his life in Boston. But his best memories reminded him of this moment.

By the time Clara called Mason over for dinner, a calmness had settled over Sullivan. Something he hadn't felt in a long time. Peace. Mason's laugh, his joy and energy, it was all infectious.

"Can't we play longer?" Mason called to Clara.

She pointed at the food. "Dinner, Mason. Now."

When Mason pouted, Sullivan got down on one knee in front of him. "Do you know what pro ballplayers need most?"

"A good bat?" Mason asked.

Sullivan chuckled. "That and food. You need to feed your muscles, make them strong."

Mason's eyes widened. "Really?"

"You bet."

Mason's expression turned eager, his smile full of joy. "Can I tell people at school I know you?"

"Would you like to tell people you know me?"

Mason nodded.

"Then, yes," Sullivan said. "Even tell them we played baseball together and I gave you this hat."

"Wow, so cool," Mason said then took off, running to the picnic table, throwing his glove into the air to hit the grass a second later. "I need to feed my muscles."

Sullivan laughed to himself, his chest warm and light. He'd been so worried all day about this meeting, but truth was, Mason was a great kid. Funny. Clever. Curious. Strong. A definite mix of him and Clara. As he watched everyone laughing and talking, he realized he'd been so selfishly focused on forgetting his life in River Rock he forgot all the good here.

After Sullivan removed his glove, he scooped up Mason's on the way over to the others. The steak dinner with salad and side dishes were set up on the long table next to the grill. Obviously, the family had big dinners like this often.

Sullivan waited with Hayes off the side while the women and Luka began filling their plates. Hayes all but glared at Luka, and Sullivan held back his laugh. Apparently, Luka wasn't raised with the good ole' boy hospitability found in River Rock.

Hayes finally turned to Sullivan. "Maisie told me and Beckett earlier what maybe we all knew all along." He gestured toward Mason. "Must have been a shock to you."

Sullivan snorted. "A shock is putting it mildly."

Hayes chuckled before his smile faded. "You did good today. Couldn't have been easy coming here, facing all this." The side of his mouth curved. "Especially with the Carter sisters watching your every move."

The thought had crossed Sullivan's mind, but he'd hoped his earlier gesture helped his case. "Ah, you're a cop. I figured they'd be on their best behavior."

"As if I can control any of them," Hayes said, dead serious.

Sullivan laughed, his gaze falling back to the table as Luka picked up his plate and began scooping up his food before Amelia. "So, when did this happen?" Sullivan asked, gesturing to Luka.

"A year after you left. They met in college," Hayes said.

Sullivan had always pegged Beckett and Amelia for marriage. "What happened with Beckett?"

Hayes scowled at Luka then gave a knowing look. "That's a good question, and one Beckett refuses to answer."

When Amelia and Maisie finished making their plates, Clara made up one for Mason and set it in front of him before quickly making her own. Sullivan scooped up more food than his stomach probably needed, but he wasn't about to pass up on a home-cooked meal. He took a seat next to Hayes. Which happened to be across from Clara. When he noticed the spot next to her was open, a part of Sullivan liked that. That Clara had never filled it with some guy no one liked and who didn't let her eat first. The other part of him didn't like she'd been alone for so long. Maybe she had one-night stands to forget too, but she deserved more than that. Hell, she deserved everything.

Breaking the silence around the table, Mason said with a full mouth, "Jordan is going to the zoo tomorrow."

"Don't talk with your mouth full," Clara rebuked, and then her voice softened as she added, "Did he tell you that at school?"

Mason chewed fast and nodded quickly. After swallowing, he continued, "Can we go? Please, please, please."

"Yes," Sullivan said. Then his brain caught up. All eyes came to him, and the silence was heavy, daunting. He cleared his throat, grabbed his napkin, and wiped his mouth. To Clara, he gently added, "Of course, only if that's all right with you. Sounds like a fun day."

Clara held his gaze for a moment, her eyes searching his. Hesitation was written into every hard line on her face. "Okay," she eventually said to him. Then she turned to Mason and added, "Would it be okay if Sullivan came with us too?"

"Yes!" Mason bounced in his seat. "I want to see the snakes and tarantulas..."

He went on and on, and everyone seemingly exhaled a long breath and returned to their dinners. Clara's gaze met Sullivan's, and her small smile told him he got this right. After all the fuck ups he'd done lately, this felt a whole lot better. Familiar. Like he was finding his old self.

Ending his speech, Mason said, "Today at school, Nathan said 'poop' in front of the whole class, and Danny farted." Mason giggled.

Maisie burst out laughing.

Clara set her fork down and her firm stare on Mason.

"We don't talk about poo or farts around the dinner table."
To Maisie, she added, "And it's not funny. It's rude."

Maisie leaned forward and winked at Mason. "It's a little
funny."

Hayes leaned over to Sullivan and said, "Welcome to the
regular show at the Carter family dinner."

Sullivan laughed, but became absorbed in Clara repri-
manding her son, Maisie still laughing, and Amelia smiling
at it all.

Yeah, he liked this.

Long after Mason had gone to bed for the night, Clara sat on
the chair next to Sullivan and stared in the crackling fire
burning brightly in the firepit surrounded by the Adiron-
dack chairs. Amelia and Luka had left long ago to her
bedroom. He'd never been one to sit around the fire. Maisie
and Hayes were inside, getting more drinks and some
snacks. But knowing Maisie, she was probably giving Clara
some time alone with Sullivan to talk. And the more Clara
thought about it, the more she knew she and Sullivan
needed to break that barrier and heal things between them,
and if anything, find a way back to friendship for Mason's
sake. "I think today went well," she said to him, breaking
through the silence.

Sullivan glanced sidelong and nodded in agreement.
"He's a cute kid. Reminds me a lot of you."

"Sometimes too much," she said with a laugh. The fire
crackled, sending embers dancing up to the dark sky full of
stars.

A long pause followed. Then, "Did I...was it—"

"You did great," she said, finding his tormented gaze on

hers. "Mason likes you. Can't ask for more than that right now."

"I suppose you're right," he said, glancing back at the fire.

She still couldn't shake the images of them playing baseball together from her mind. The sweetness of it. Hell, the wish that maybe all this could work out and Mason would finally have a father figure in his life. *One step at a time,* she reminded herself, not letting herself get too carried away with whimsical thoughts that may never be. But even so, it was easy to remember the Sullivan she'd loved. This guy tonight seemed so much like him. His legs were stretched out, crossed at the ankles, relaxed, and enjoying the quiet night. "How long has it been since you've done something like this?" she asked.

"Seven years."

"Seriously? Seven years?"

The light from the fire was impressively bright, revealing the chiseled lines of his cheekbones. "Life is different in Boston," he explained, gaze on the sky. "Not so quiet. And when we travel for games, we always play in big cities. I don't get the chance to get out to places where the city lights don't hide the stars."

She looked to the sky herself, spotting the milky way. Over the years, many of her old high school friends had moved away with big city dreams. She'd never had those dreams herself, loving small-town life. The old Sullivan she knew would have hated the big city too. She figured she better get to know *this* Sullivan. "Do you like the big city?" she asked.

"Parts of it," he said. "Some parts, I don't."

She smiled, dropping her head to the side to watch his expression. "Like the bars?"

The side of his mouth curved before he glanced her way, lifting an eyebrow. "You saw the tabloid article, then?"

She nodded. Everyone saw all the articles about him. Every week, on a new issue in the grocery store line. "What's going on with all of that? The bar fights and stuff?" And, of course, by "stuff," she totally meant women.

Obviously picking up on that, Sullivan's mouth quirked up at the corner again. "Does the *stuff* wear dresses and high heels?"

She sent her gaze to the fire. "It's none of my business. You don't have to talk about it. It's just..."

"Just what?"

She felt his stare. "You were always a one-woman type of guy. What changed?"

"Nothing," he said in a quiet voice. She dared to look at him then, and his jaw was clenched, tension creasing the lines around his eyes while he watched the fire burn. "The women, they're a distraction."

"From?" she pressed, not even sure why she wanted to know the answer so bad.

The heat from the fire became all-encompassing as he drew in the longest, deepest breath then blew it out through his nose. "From the shit that gets heavy in my head."

She froze, shocked by his answer. Of all the things she had expected him to say, that certainly wasn't it. *For fun. Because I don't want anything serious.* Something like that, not anything deep.

At the silence, he turned his head to the side, watching her closely. "Distractions help me take a break from that."

"I suppose they would," she agreed gently. She had seen the guy she loved fade when his mom passed away, but he was lost forever when his father's abuse started. But right here, right now, she could almost see the guy he'd been when his mother was alive. The good guy, the guy who wouldn't simply vanish from someone's life so cruelly. "What about this bar fight that got you suspended?"

"It never should have happened," he said, looking back to the sky with a heavy sigh. "I'm careful not to drink too much, to always stay in control, but that night, my control slipped."

She took a guess. "Because of your dad dying?"

"I suspect my dad's death had something to do with it, yeah." The shame on his face was more punishment than anyone should endure, and the orange hue from the fire detailed every bit of it. "We were leaving the bar, me and a bunch of teammates, and we came across an asshole fighting with his girlfriend. He was screaming at her, and then he pushed her, and she fell." He stopped to take a deep breath before continuing. "I didn't know them. I had no business interfering. But something in my head snapped, and I acted before I even knew what was happening."

"Wait," Clara said, trying to understand. "Why didn't you say that the guy was hurting his girlfriend? I'd say that's forgivable. You were protecting her."

"Because I'm no better, Clara," Sullivan said, dryly. He turned his head then, revealing many years of pain in his eyes. "I put my hands on someone in violence, in rage. That is unforgivable."

She tried to see it his way, but failed. "No, you were giving the guy a taste of his own medicine. Seriously, Sullivan, people would have sided with you." She watched him for a moment, looking for a single flicker of agreement with her on his expression. Trying to understand, she asked, "So, instead of explaining that, you took the suspension?"

"That's right."

She processed, scenting the piney aroma from the trees

hugging the firepit. Nothing felt...*right*. Something was missing. She sat up straight, scooting to the end of her chair to face him fully. "Why are you home, Sullivan?" she asked.

His brows drew together. "You already know why. To get my head right."

She considered all this again, but something seemed off. "I know what you told me. A bar fight led to a suspension, and you came home to deal with your past because of the fight. But to avoid all of that, all you had to do was tell the truth about what happened. So, again, *why* are you here?"

Their gazes held before he looked back at the fire. It seemed like he wasn't going to answer her, but then she almost wished he hadn't. "When I sobered up that next day at the police station, I knew I was on my way to becoming him."

"Your father?"

"Yes," he said slowly.

Clara's heart squeezed painfully, her breath all but gone.

Before she could even think up a reply, he added, "Of course, not completely. I still think the guy I hit deserved it. But I realized I became the very thing I hate. I pushed all the bad shit down deep enough that I felt nothing. Just rage. Until it all exploded." He turned his head again, torment swirling in the depths of his eyes, and said oh-so softly, "My dad did that until there was nothing left of him, until only rage lived in the spots that were once good. So, that's why I'm here, Clara. To face the shit that makes me feel uncomfortable so that doesn't happen to me."

The world seemed to slow as coldness swept across her. Not knowing what to say, she looked to the fire because, just like that, the years vanished. This was the Sullivan she did know, and she, behind all the hurt and worry for Mason's well-being, loved this man. But he was drowning in the dark misery and desperately wanted a way out, but unable to find it.

"Clara."

His soft voice pulled her focus to his warm, gentle eyes.

"I'm sorry for leaving you the way I did." His voice blistered. "I'm sorry I wasn't strong enough to be what you needed."

Tears welled in her eyes, and nothing could stop them from rolling down her cheeks. For as long as she could remember, she'd wanted an explanation, an apology. Now she had those things, but only one truth remained: they'd both done their best in a terrible situation that no one deserved. As much as she wanted to blame Sullivan for leaving and breaking her heart, she couldn't. Her aching heart reached for him. "I'm sorry I wasn't strong enough to help you."

Everything around Clara vanished. The firepit gone. The trees gone. Only a deep-rooted, forgotten love remained.

At whatever crossed her expression, emotion touched Sullivan's gaze as he reached for her hand and said softly, "Clara—"

The backdoor slamming closed snapped Clara's hand away before Sullivan could take it. Immediately, she was hit by the smoky aroma of the fire. Unexpected heat flooded her, and she couldn't decide if she was happy for the interruption or not.

"Who's ready for S'mores?" Maisie asked on her way toward the firepit with Hayes by her side carrying the metal marshmallow sticks.

"Me," Clara said, jumping out of her chair to sit next to Maisie. But, no matter the distance between them, she felt Sullivan's heated stare, right down into her soul, begging her to come back.

7

Hours after Sullivan left, Clara tucked herself away in bed, but she couldn't sleep, tossing and turning, feeling like she needed to hear what Sullivan had wanted to say before Maisie interrupted them. She considered calling. But that didn't seem like enough. Instead, with Amelia keeping an eye on a sleeping Mason, Clara hopped in her car and hit the road. When she pulled into the long driveway leading to Sullivan's apartment, the gravel crunched beneath her tires. She rolled to a stop off to the side of the weathered red building. The house to the right was bathed in darkness. Old man Bart, sound asleep.

Raw emotions led her feet as she exited the car and then headed up the steps of the barn. When she reached the worn old door, she froze, a million thoughts crossing her mind. The night lay still around her. *I need to say more. I don't hate you. I hate your father for what he did to us. I hate that you're still carrying around all this pain after all these years. I hate that after all the love we had, we ended like we did. I want to forgive you. I want to move on. What did you want to tell me?*

She drew in a long, deep breath, hoping to hell she got this right, and then she knocked.

No response.

She knocked again, and when the door opened, Clara only *just* managed to stop her mouth from dropping open.

Sullivan's brows went up. "Clara? What's wrong?"

He opened the door wider, and a slow-building heat rolled over her. Sullivan had always been a good-looking guy, but now, he was pure man, with a body that looked cut from a fitness magazine. His hair was wet from an obvious shower, telling her he couldn't sleep either, and a towel was wrapped around his wide bare shoulders. Her fingers tingled to reach out and touch him, and her breath became ragged as she let her gaze follow a path down his squared chest to his six-pack to that sexy V at his hips to his gray sweatpants that left absolutely nothing to the imagination as to what he had beneath them. And she really, *really* liked what he had. Scratch that, she suddenly really, *really* wanted what he had.

She swallowed deeply, and by the time she glanced back up, Sullivan's eyes were hot and hungry.

A beat passed.

She could nearly taste the energy pinging between them. The heat burning. The want to make all that had gone so wrong better. "Sullivan—"

That's all she managed before he had her in his arms, kicking the door shut behind them. She went willingly, forgetting what she'd wanted to hear. Because this was both an apology and an acknowledgment of them taking back all they had lost. His woodsy-scented shampoo infused the air when his mouth met hers, and she tumbled into everything the kiss promised. His kiss was familiar, and yet different, older, wiser, more patient and knowledgeable. Every slide of his tongue and deep, passionate press of his lips had her reaching for more.

When he finally broke the kiss, long minutes later, they were both breathless. He cupped her face, heady emotion dancing in his eyes. "I love kissing you, Clara. In fact, I want to kiss you until we forget why we shouldn't be kissing, but I don't want to hurt you again."

"I won't let you hurt me again," she told him, dead serious. "I'm not that young girl who blindly loved you." She slid her hands up his huge arms, feeling each muscle flex under her touch. "Your dad stole something from us. I want it back."

Sullivan pressed his forehead against hers. "I'm not staying in River Rock. When my suspension is over, I'm going home. This can't last."

She cupped his face now, bringing his tormented gaze back to her. For all the confusion and the worry of wondering what to say to him, now it became all too clear. "We were never meant to last, but we can choose how we end it this time. To take back what was stolen from us, and give ourselves what we should have had—a proper goodbye. To finally heal all that went wrong. Then we can finally put all this behind us and go on with our lives."

He watched her closely, then all the hesitation faded from his eyes. Their lips met again as his agreement, and there was nothing soft about it. The kiss was rough and spoke of years of heartbreak. Years of pain they could never recover from. And *this,* this was their time to heal.

When he broke the kiss again, he spun her around, his strong chest to her back. She shivered, sliding her hands down his thighs as his kiss traveled over her neck. A soft moan spilled free when his hands working their way under her top. "You're so beautiful, Clara." His voice a low rumble in her ear, sliding his strong hand across her stomach. "Somehow even more beautiful now."

She felt those words ripple across her. Felt his touch right down into her soul. Here, between them, there was unthinkable pain. Hard truths. But there had once been love, so much love. She twisted around and her mouth met his, and she kissed him, slow and easy. His woodsy aroma swirled around her as she became overwhelmed by him. His warm full lips were just as she remembered, like no time had passed. She kept wanting to pull back, to see reason, but the more she kissed him, the harder it became to pull away. Until all that lingered was *need*. It lived in the deepest parts of her heart that longed for his touch again.

Soon, he had her shirt off and unhooked her bra, revealing her breasts to him. He cupped her, kissed her, teased her nipples, sucking them up to the roof of his mouth, until all she knew was hot pleasure. She moaned against his touch imprinted on her skin. He was more confident now, more experienced, and she relished in his powerful embrace.

This time, when he leaned away, something on her stomach caught his eye. She followed his gaze then watched as he traced the three stretch marks on the side of her belly.

"From Mason?" he asked.

She nodded and couldn't speak when she saw the sheer emotion in his eyes.

Not wanting to talk, only wanting to feel, her lips met his again, and his pants were soon gone. And then hers did too. Until they were bared to each other, except for the condom between them. He gathered her in his arms, laid her out on the bed, and slid her beneath him. She cupped his face, like she'd done the night he took her virginity. They'd both been nervous, unsure, and yet once together, everything made sense.

Hovering over her, resting his weight on one arm, he brushed his thumb against her cheek, the side of his mouth curving oh-so deliciously. "I used to dream of seeing you like this again."

"Reality is better." Emotion and pulsating desire consumed her as she slid her hand over the hard muscles of his butt cheek and wrapped her legs around his hips, guiding him inside her.

His low groan washed over her, and then he began moving. This time, when his mouth met hers, the kiss was different. All-consuming as he swept her away to a place where they'd once lived. A safe space full of trust and of possibilities. Each movement was slow but with the intent to tease and to offer pleasure. He thrust as if he meant for her to feel all of him, and she did—every single glorious inch, until her back was arching and her toes were curling. He tangled one hand into her hair. With the other, he pinned her hip to the blanket below. His eyes—oh, his eyes simmered with hunger.

"Sullivan," she moaned.

He answered her with a low growl. His thrusts becoming harder, faster, as he grew harder insider her. They moved together, a steady rhythm, slapping skin against skin, his moans echoing hers. Until the pleasure became too much— so much, so good—taking her to the place only he'd ever taken her. Right over the edge, where she utterly let go. Only then did he follow her.

Sometime later, she found herself lying on her side, spooned by him. She wiggled back into him, catching her breath, and his arms tightened further around her.

A sweet, comfortable silence settled in. One Clara didn't

want to let go of. How many times had she wished and prayed that Sullivan would hold her like this again? For this one moment, she let her guards fall and allowed her young heart to relish in his safe hold.

Until he broke the silence. "What happened after I left?" he asked.

Reminded of the past, she processed his question, realized she'd heard him right, then flipped over to face him. His eyes were soft, curious, his hair damp with sweat. "Why are you asking that?"

His voice was sleepy, rough. "I want to know what you went through."

Thinking that right now, for Mason and to finally heal, they needed only the truth between them, she indulged him. "It wasn't pretty," she told him honestly. "Are you sure you want to know?"

"Yes," he said, adamant.

It occurred to her that while she was doing her own type of healing to mend past hurts; he was too. Because she knew he needed it, she let herself go back into the past, to a day she'd thought she'd never recover from.

Clara pulled up to Sullivan's childhood home. Tears flooded her face as she stood on the front yard, staring at the house that had once held so much love. Why did his mother have to die? Why couldn't they cure cancer? Why did Sullivan have to leave?

Her feet moved, bringing her to the front door. Her knuckles knocked. Everything felt dream-like, slow and unbelievable. No way this could be her life.

The front door opened. Sullivan's dad remained rooted in the doorway, his eyes bloodshot and his hair long and ragged. "Sullivan's gone," she heard herself saying. At Kurtis' silence, she yelled, "He's gone. Did you hear me? He left me because of you. He's gone!"

Kurtis simply blinked.

Anger boiled inside her. She clenched her fists at her side. "Now you have nothing to say? You were so cruel to him, but now that he's gone, you're silent? How fucking dare you? Your wife would be ashamed of what you've become."

"It's good he's gone," Kurtis growled. "Don't ever come back here." He began to close the door.

That barely in-check rage burst wide open, and before Clara could stop herself, her clenched fist tightened, and using all her strength, she punched him, hearing a loud crack. Her knuckles crunched, and she screamed against the pain blasting through her fingers. Blood poured from Kurtis' nose as she screamed at him, "I will never forgive you."

Her cries faded from her ears as Sullivan asked, "You punched him?"

She blinked, realizing she'd told him everything without filters, and noted the tightness around his eyes. "I did, and I broke a couple fingers too."

She held up her hand and showed him the two fingers. He examined them, running his thumb across the crooked parts before his gaze met hers again. "What happened after that?"

With a sigh, she tucked her hand between her cheek and the pillow. "I guess your neighbors saw, or had been watching, probably because they worried about me, and they ran over and pulled me away then called the cops."

"Did the cops do anything?"

She shook her head. "They had to take me to the station for a report, but of course, they never pressed charges. For one, your dad didn't want me charged, and Hayes' father was totally on my side."

Sullivan watched her for a long moment. His expression

revealing nothing. He eventually asked, "What made you go to see him in the first place?'

"Honestly, there were a million reasons. I was so angry and hurt that you were gone, and at the time, I wanted him to know that. To know that it was all his fault you were gone. That your mother would have been so ashamed of him. That I was ashamed of him." She hesitated, trying to put into words what had been an emotional mess at the time. "I wanted him to feel accountable, I guess, but things changed after that day."

"Why?"

Warmth filled her chest, and she smiled, hoping Sullivan saw all of her happiness. "Because I found out I was pregnant with Mason. It's weird, you know, but the timing of all of it was crazy. The day before I found out, I booked a plane ticket to come out to see you. I thought if you could just see me, then we could make it work."

His brows rose. "You came out to Boston?"

"No, I never made it, because the night before my flight, Amelia convinced me to take a pregnancy test, and it came back positive. Everything changed in an instant." She paused, holding his gaze, knowing what she was about to say would hurt. "Because someone mattered more than you."

"Mason," he said gently.

She nodded. "Mason. So, I decided to call you once more to let you know about the pregnancy."

"But a woman answered."

"She sure did," she agreed, her heart lodged into her throat. "That's when I knew I needed to accept that you were never coming back for me. I decided then to let you go and let you live out your dream in Boston. You deserved that happiness, and I had Mason." A thousand emotions flashed over his face as he rolled onto his back and looked up at the ceiling. One minute ticked by then another. She couldn't stand the silence anymore. "Please tell me what you're thinking."

A beat passed then he turned his head, the side of his mouth curving slightly. "I'm thinking that I'm annoyed."

"Annoyed?"

He chuckled, shaking his head slowly, then gathered her in his arms until he hovered above her. "Yes, Slugger, annoyed that you punched my bastard father in the face and I didn't get the chance to see it." She laughed, and he pressed his lips to the top of her head before making direct eye contact again. "I'm sorry, Clara. I'm sorry I hurt you. I'm sorry for being a coward and not taking your calls seven years ago. I'm sorry for the anger you endured after I left and for how lonely and scared you must have felt. Most of all, I'm sorry I wasn't there for you and Mason."

She cupped his face, hoping he heard her. "Honestly, Sullivan, I'm done with apologies and regrets. The past is the past. You're here now. Let's make this good for Mason and move on from the rest."

He whispered against her lips, "One day at a time."

"One day at a time." Then she claimed his mouth.

8

The next morning, after dressing for the day and over hot coffee, Clara spent the morning hours reviewing the contracts and drawing up her counteroffers. Of course, their lawyer would review her requests before they sent the contract back to Ronnie and the other distributors, but she knew what they needed for the brewery to survive. And for Mason, the brewery needed to kick some serious butt. For Pops, her grandfather who'd loved his beer and left his life savings to support this venture, Clara couldn't stop pushing until they got what they needed to make this business successful. She felt the pressure weighing on her shoulders, but everything would work out. There was simply no other choice.

Leaving Mason to finish getting dressed upstairs, and feeling tired from last night with Sullivan, she headed downstairs for her second cup of coffee. When she woke up this morning, an unexpected peace washed over her. The tension that always lived in the center of her chest had lessened. And while she knew the healing with Sullivan was for Mason's sake, she hadn't quite realized how much she needed it to. To hear an apology, to understand *why* Sullivan had given up on her, were all things she didn't know she needed. She finished stirring in the cream and sugar into her coffee when a knock came at the front door. She whisked it open to reveal a sight she'd seen many times, many years ago.

Sullivan greeted her with a warm smile and a sweet peck on the cheek. "Ready to go?" he asked.

Her belly fluttered right alongside her heart. Sullivan always seemed to have a way of looking good without even trying. Handsome and charming and all the things in between, he wore jeans and a white T-shirt, his hair rustled and unstyled. He looked like a dream come true. If she was being honest, it was her dream come true. Before she could respond to his question, a blur of beige shorts and a blue T-shirt rushed by as Mason ran outside into a clear sunny morning without a cloud in the sky. Clara shook her head at her rambunctious son and finally answered Sullivan, "That's a definite yes."

"Then, let's be on our way," Sullivan said, stepping out of the way.

Clara quickly put her coffee in a to-go mug, grabbed her purse off the hook on the wall, shut the door behind her, then snatched up the booster seat she'd left on the porch last night.

Right as Mason opened the back door, Sullivan called, "Mason, buddy, hold up."

Mason whirled back to Sullivan, confusion in his eyes.

Sullivan jogged down the porch steps and then went down to one knee, making eye contact. "Whenever ladies are with us, we open the door for them first before we get in."

Mason gave a quizzical look. "Why?"

"You love your mama, right?" Sullivan asked gently.

Mason nodded. "Yeah."

"You want your mama to feel special?"

Another nod.

Sullivan's smile warmed as he gestured back at Clara. "This is one way we can show her that we're thinking of her and appreciate all she does for us."

"Oh," Mason said, examining Clara with his little brows furrowed. Then he smiled big and ran around Sullivan to open the passenger-side door. "Get in, Mama."

Clara's heart tripped as she was fighting back the tears. "Thank you, sweetie." He was gone a second later, taking the booster seat with him to the back seat and was fastening his seat belt. She swallowed back the emotion and said quietly to Sullivan, "Thanks for that." Of course, she'd taught Mason manners over the years, but it occurred to her now, she'd never asked for those manners for herself. She wasn't sure how she felt about that either. When did she stop thinking about herself?

Sullivan slowly rose, the heat of his body so close. His eyes were steady, and Clara got lost in that for a moment, hoping he'd come even closer. "You'll tell me if I overstep?" He lifted a shoulder. "Just felt like I—"

"Did the right thing," she said with a firm nod. "You didn't overstep."

His smile widened. "Good."

Sullivan's woodsy cologne infused the air, bringing Clara back to last night when all she smelled was him, all she felt was him, all she wanted was *him*. Her nipples puckered, and she immediately stepped back, putting some distance between her and all of Sullivan's heat. His devilish smile said he read right through her.

"Come on," Mason called, bouncing in the seat. "Let's go!"

Glad for the distraction, Clara shook her head at Mason and told Sullivan, "Manners are a work in progress."

Sullivan winked. "For most people."

He shut the door behind her then trotted around the hood of the truck to hop in next to her. As he started the ignition, she glanced back at Mason, who was smiling ear to ear, and her gaze fell on Sullivan, who had the same grin. Even she felt the beaming happiness on her face. Life could be a real bitch sometimes, but then, it could take wonderful, surprising turns. And for all the hard times when every- thing had seemed so difficult, Clara settled back into the seat, sighed, and smiled too.

"Can we see the tigers first?" Mason asked from the back seat as Sullivan drove off. "No, the lions." A pause. "No, the monkeys. Wait." His babbling continued in a blur of words and indecisiveness.

Sullivan leaned over with a grin. "Is it always like this?"

"Always." Clara smiled back.

Staying true to himself, Mason kept talking the entire afternoon at Denver's zoo, and Sullivan kept up. Mason's excitement was infectious, and Clara had seen an unex- pected shift in Sullivan. He'd turned into a big kid who seemed to enjoy the zoo as much as Mason did. After they had lunch at the Lion café, it occurred to her that Sullivan probably hadn't done anything like this since before his mother passed away.

"I love the lemurs," Mason said, clutching onto Clara's hand.

"They are very cute," she agreed.

Mason smiled then scooped up Sullivan's hand and asked, "Did you like the lemurs too, Sullian?"

Sullivan looked to their held hands for a beat then his smiled warmed. "Yeah, buddy, I loved the lemurs. Those silly monkeys too."

"Mama calls me a monkey all the time," Mason exclaimed with a laugh, then dropped their hands and went running down the pathway.

"Not too far ahead," Clara called after him.

Sullivan laughed softly then said to Clara, "It's safe to say he likes the zoo, huh?"

"He loves everything," Clara replied. With Mason gone, her hand brushed Sullivan's. She had to fight the instinct to take it. Today felt like the very dream she'd had before Mason was born. Doing things just like this, spending the afternoon at the zoo with Sullivan and their child. Once Mason came, she couldn't think about dreams like that. But the truth was, and always would be, she could only imagine that dream happening with Sullivan. And there was a part of her heart that never wanted to let this moment go.

Sullivan was silent next to her, a quiet peace on his face.

To gauge where his head was at, she said, "You're good at this, you know." She tucked her thumbs in the back pockets of her jeans to keep her hands to herself. "When did you become so good with kids?"

"Seven years playing pro ball," he answered, his hand closest to her shoved into his pocket like he was trying to control himself as well. "Kids come with that territory." His gaze turned a little unsure. "But thanks—I appreciate your approval. I definitely feel out of my element here."

"You'd never know it," Clara said seriously. "I've never seen Mason grab someone's hand like that other than with Amelia and Maisie."

Sullivan looked to Mason, who stopped at the flamingos,

his gaze thoughtful, contemplating. "We should tell him the truth."

Clara slowed and stopped near the capybara habitat. Mason was still watching the flamingos, and while Clara kept him in her sight, she asked Sullivan, "Are you sure you're ready for that? It's a commitment forever. There is no going back after that. Again, we don't have to rush this."

Sullivan paused, considering. "It's a secret I don't want to keep anymore." With a sigh, he leaned against the wooden fence, arms resting on top. "There's been a lot in my life that I've gotten wrong." He hesitated again then shook his head slowly before his emotion-filled eyes met Clara's. "Mason is something I got right without even knowing it. He's family. *My family*. I want him to know that. If you're okay with it, that's is."

Now, Clara paused. Every alarm inside her blared. Everything would change after that. Mason's safe bubble would no longer only belong to her. Sullivan and her would co-parent. He'd be involved in all decisions and could hurt Mason. "This is hard for me," she admitted. "It's only ever been us."

"I know," Sullivan said then took her hand, squeezing tight. "But things have changed now. I've changed. And I'll keep changing and doing what I have to do to be a good role model in Mason's life. You've got my promise on that." He leaned down, bringing his eyes level with hers. "I won't hurt him. I won't leave him."

That's when she saw the truth written all over his face. He needed Mason as much as she did. Mason was the good, the sweet, the special that he'd never seen coming. "Okay, we'll tell him."

"Tonight?"

She nodded. "Tonight."

"Sullian," Mason yelled, running back over to them. "What is *that*?"

Sullivan glanced into the habit and frowned. "That's a giant guinea pig."

Clara laughed. "It's a Capybara, not a giant guinea pig."

Sullivan pointed at the Capybara. "Sure looks like a giant guinea pig to me."

"Me, too." Mason burst out laughing, grabbing Sullivan's hand to tug him forward. "Look at the size of its poo."

Clara stayed back a little, watched them talk boy-talk that she would never understand. But one thing she did understand was their smiles that felt so true and honest, giving off so much warmth she felt it all around her.

❦

Once they arrived home, Clara made a quick spaghetti dinner and Sullivan helped with the sauce. He'd never been so domesticated in his life, and yet, oddly, it all felt very comfortable, a life he'd once had with his family. He knew the difficult questions and answers ahead of him, but for the first time in his life, he felt like he was on the exact right path. He'd come home to make amends, and he was making them. They had planned to tell Mason the truth after dinner, but he had looked tired after the long afternoon, so Clara thought the conversation should wait until tomorrow. Sullivan agreed. After that, he easily fell into the rhythm of Clara's and Mason's evening routine, and before bed, he built a blanket fort with Mason and they all watched a Disney movie.

When the movie wrapped up, Clara began dismantling the fort and said, "Off to bed, buddy."

Sullivan felt a tug on his shirt. "Sullian, Sullian. Come on, read me a story."

He glanced back, got hit with those sweet eyes, and felt trapped in the best way possible. Nerves about putting Mason to bed *alone* danced in his gut, but he clamped down on them and followed Mason up the staircase.

When they entered his bedroom, Mason turned back, awaiting Sullivan's instruction. "You'll have to help me here, buddy," Sullivan said. "I've got no idea what to do."

"It's easy," said Mason, running to his dresser. He grabbed plaid pants and a T-shirt. "Pajamas, wash my face and hands, brush my teeth. And then a book." He picked one up and handed it to Sullivan. The front read: TEAM-WORK BY ROBERT MUNSCH. Sullivan tucked the book under his arm. "Okay, do I wait here for you?"

"Yep," Mason said, running toward the door. "Mom always says to brush my teeth twice to get all the sugar bugs."

"Then, brush your teeth twice."

With Mason off getting ready for bed, he thought back to what his mom used to do for him. Sullivan turned on the nightstand lamp and then hit the switch for the main light. He pulled the sheets back, then sat on the side of the bed where his mother used to sit when she'd read him a story. Warmth touched all the cold places in his chest.

"Reeeeeady," Mason yelled, charging toward the bed.

Sullivan shoved his thoughts away then settled in next to Mason so he could see the pictures of the story. As he read, Mason listened to every single word and laughed a bunch. A warm comfort slid over Sullivan. He felt like he'd missed so much, so many happy moments, all because he'd run from the pain he couldn't face.

It wasn't until he closed the book and rose that Mason finally spoke again. "Are you my dad?"

Sullivan locked his knees. Then Clara entered the room with a soft smile he thought was meant to reassure him, though even she looked unsteady. Sullivan both wanted to run and drop to the floor all at the same time. He turned to Mason and stared again into those eyes that looked so much like his mother's and realized all this was simple. The truth was good, felt good, and felt right. Sullivan sat back next to Mason. "Yeah, buddy, I am."

Mason smiled. "Thought so."

Clara came over and knelt next to the bed. "You're so clever, sweetie." She rustled up his hair. "How did you know?"

"Sullian brought you flowers," Mason explained. "Mommies and Daddies do that."

Clara's smile warmed. "They sure do. You're such a smart cookie." She tickled Mason's side, sending him into a fit of laughter.

When that laughter died, Mason looked directly at Sullivan. "Why were you gone?"

Sullivan hesitated, unsure how to answer.

In that slight pause, Clara interjected, "Remember how we talk sometimes about how people's mental health is important?"

"Yeah," Mason said with a nod.

Clara brushed the hair back from Mason's face, her voice as gentle as ever. "Sullivan needed help with his mental health before he could be the best dad to you."

"Oh," Mason said then set those clever eyes on Sullivan. "But you're okay now?"

Sullivan barely got air into his chest but managed, "I'm getting better day by day." Of course, the answers were far more complicated, and when older, Mason was owed those answers, but for now, this explanation seemed right. Of course Clara knew how to handle all this. An unexpected release of tension hit as he added, "And I'd really like to be in your life now, if you're okay with that."

Mason jumped up and threw his arms around Sullivan, catching him by surprise. Until he remembered what a hug like this felt like. A hug so honest and sweet and loving. He tightened his arms around Mason when Mason said, "I can't wait to tell everyone at school that my dad is a professional baseball player."

Sullivan laughed and hugged him tighter for as long as he'd allow.

Which wasn't long. Mason wiggled out of his arms, climbing back into the bed, and his smile lit up the room. "Snug as a bug in a rug," he told Sullivan.

Sullivan arched a brow. "Snug as a bug in a rug?"

"That's how you tuck me in," Mason explained, digging his fingers in around his legs. "Snug as a bug in a rug."

Sullivan breathed past the hit to his chest as the memory of his mother doing that to him at bedtime slid into his mind. Something Clara knew very well. He'd shared that memory of his mother with her once. And her soft smile told him that's exactly why she'd kept the ritual going. "You're right. I can't forget that." Sullivan rose, tucking Mason in tight. "Snug as a bug in a rug."

Mason grinned. "All tight?"

"All tight." Sullivan smiled, feeling heat radiating through his chest.

Once Sullivan backed away, Clara sidled next to the bed and kissed Mason's forehead. "Love you, buddy. If you've got any more questions for either Sullivan or me, just ask them, okay?"

Mason yawned. "Okay."

Sullivan turned off the lamp, remembering back to all the times his mother would blow him a kiss before shutting the door close.

When he followed Clara out into the hall, she adjusted the door and said, "You have to leave the door open a little. The light from the hallway kills the monsters."

He chuckled. "Safety first."

"Exactly," she said and gestured down the stairs. "I've got drinks for us outside on the porch."

"I bet we both could use one."

She agreed with a nod, and he followed her down the steps then out into the warm night, the porch light spilling over them. She sat first on the porch swing and he followed, grabbing his beer that sat next to her wine. A moment passed before he spoke. "I think that went well."

She finished her sip of wine and nodded. "It did. Kids are amazingly resilient. I'm sure he'll have a thousand more questions, but at this age, everything is very simple like you saw. He thinks you're cool, and I have no doubt he'll like telling people he has a dad. As much as Amelia and Maisie have tried to fill that role, there is no replacing a father's role in a child's life."

He nodded. All the years Sullivan had missed, all that time. He glanced down at his boots he'd left on the porch planks. Boots that were so different from the fancy shoes he wore when he went out in Boston. He'd never realized how much he missed this. The countryside. The dirty boots. The quiet nights on the porch. "Now that Mason knows, where do we go from here?"

She finished her sip then rested her wineglass on her thigh before setting her hard stare on him. "I suppose that's the question, isn't it?"

He gave a slow nod.

"Well, is living here in River Rock out of the question?" she asked with a laugh, obviously joking.

"No, it's not," he said, dead serious. Her laughter died, and he reached for her hand, sliding the strength of his along her delicate fingers. "Since I've come back, I feel happier than I've felt in a long time. Today, well, today was amazing." And finally saying what had been lying between them, he asked, "Aren't you feeling that same way?"

She glanced down to their entwined hands. "I am happy." When her eyes lifted, there was unrelenting sadness there. "But I also can't live in this happy bubble where I only think of myself. Yes, things have been amazing. Yes, I've dreamed of having this with us and with having you in our lives. But you don't live in River Rock, Sullivan. And I know, while you're doing a lot to help yourself, that living here is not something you want."

He processed that. "What if what I wanted before has changed now?"

Her eyes searched his. "Then, you can change your mind, but..." Her long pause spoke of remaining pain. "I can't make that decision with you. Not this time. I..." Her voice hitched as she slowly shook her head. "I can't go through all that again. So, while I will continue to protect Mason's best interests, I also know you're good for him. Having a daddy is important, and it makes me happy you're in his life. But, as for *us*, anything beyond saying goodbye at the end of your suspension, is just not in my capabilities right now."

And that was maybe the saddest part of all. Sullivan had made mistakes. Big ones. But none more terrible than what he'd done to her heart. "I understand."

She squeezed his fingers, and as she did with everyone,

she attempted to make him feel better about it all. "I need this time together as much as you do. I appreciate every second of it, but in all this, I can only think of Mason. I feel like we're in a really good place. We can't screw that up by going too deep and drowning again."

"Then, we'll stay afloat," he promised. Mason was at the top of his list of priorities, but so was Clara, and now he knew a hard truth. He wasn't doing enough to heal her heart. Not even close. And that needed to change.

9

A couple of days later, after dropping Mason off at school, Clara returned home to focus on the brewery. She'd never sent the counteroffers she'd drawn up, and the distributors were checking in to see if she'd made a decision, as was her lawyer. But Clara remained hesitant to send anything in yet, so she delayed by saying she needed more time to review the contracts. Her demands were high, and she needed to be sure she wasn't asking for too much and they'd all walk away. She was well into responding to emails when she received a text from Sullivan: CAN YOU MAKE IT OUT TO COORS FIELD THIS MORNING?

She fired off her response: ARE YOU GOING TO TELL ME WHY I NEED TO GO THERE?

YOU'LL SEE WHEN YOU GET HERE. CAN WE MEET IN AN HOUR? IF POSSIBLE, BRING YOUR SISTERS.

Confused but growing curious, she responded: MAKE IT AN HOUR AND A BIT. I NEED TO WRANGLE THEM UP.

PERFECT. SEE YOU SOON.

She sent quick texts to Maisie and Amelia, asking if they

could join her, which they agreed to after sending many questions. Questions that didn't last long when, on the drive into Denver, Clara filled her sisters in on Sullivan and Mason's talk last night.

"Kids are smarter than people give them credit for," Clara said after she'd caught them up and they'd arrived at Coors Field. Located only two blocks from Union Station, the Coors Field building was designed to impress with its curved front architecture and clock tower. Once she parked, she stepped out into the cloudy day and shut the car door behind her, finding the parking lot empty and Sullivan's truck nowhere in sight. "Mason's young," she told her sisters. "He doesn't really understand why Sullivan hasn't been there this whole time. He's only happy that he now has a dad and that his dad plays professional baseball. It's simple for him right now."

Maisie met her at the hood, giving a small shrug. "It might not always be that simple."

"I'm sure it won't be," she agreed, tucking her car keys into her front pocket. "I've got no doubt his little mind will fill up with questions that need answers, and I'll—Sullivan and I will get them answered."

"I think that's really great," Amelia said, sidling up to them. "Mason seems really happy when Sullivan's around. And I feel like Sullivan's really done the work to be a good role model for him. You gotta give him credit for that. He's definitely not the sly dog we all thought he was when he first came back. He's really changed. Or at least looking to better himself."

"Agreed," Clara said.

Maisie added, "Besides, you can always take Mason to Doctor Stevens if you feel he needs to talk things out with a professional."

Clara nodded. "Yeah, I've considered that. I've got a close eye on him. He'll be all right, but if he's not, getting professional help will be at the top of my priority list." At Maisie's probing gaze, Clara added, "What?"

"I guess I'm just wondering if you and Sullivan are all right. You haven't really said anything about you guys."

Clara paused until it became clear it was nearly impossible to explain. "It's a lot, you know? There's a big past there with lots of confusing parts, and I feel like we're really beginning to heal. But again, going slow through all this is the only way forward."

"You've both been through a lot," Amelia said in agreement. "There's no need to rush any of this. I think it's great you're figuring all this out for Mason. He'll be a happier kid for it." She nudged Clara's shoulder. "And if I may say, you seem pretty happy too."

As a couple pigeons landed a few feet away, pecking at the pavement, Clara drew in a long, deep breath. "You know what? I am happy. I mean, when does someone get the chance to rewrite their past and take something that went so wrong and make it better?"

"Not very often," Maisie said.

"Exactly," Clara said with a nod. "Things are moving in the right direction, and I'm grateful for that." Needing to get the show on the road and find out why Sullivan had called them there, Clara gestured her sisters forward. "So, how about we go see why Sullivan asked us to come here?"

Maisie linked arms with Clara. "Yes, let's do just that."

Her sisters fell into step with her as they strode through the large parking lot and made it to the main gate, where Sullivan was waiting along with a security guard.

"Good, you're here," he said by way of greeting.

His bright eyes spoke of mischief. "We are, so can you let us in on the secret now?"

"Let me show you." Sullivan grinned.

The security guard locked the gate behind them then led them toward the concession stand in the large open space with concrete on the floor and metal construction beams exposed in the roof. The stadium was crawling with workers getting ready for the baseball game tonight, where the Boston Red Sox were playing the Colorado Rockies, something Maisie had learned on the drive to Coors Field.

"I'll leave you here," the security guard said when they reached the microbrewery located behind the right-field stands.

"Thanks," Sullivan said.

The security guard flicked the rim of his cowboy hat then headed off to the right. "Thanks again for that autograph for my kid."

"Anytime," Sullivan said.

Clara rocked back on her heels, inhaling the ozone-like smell of cement and metal, glancing around the stadium. "So, we are here because..."

Maisie's gasp suddenly filled the air.

Clara quickly followed her gaze and immediately understood why she was so surprised. Next to the microbrewery was a booth with Foxy Diva merchandise. Hayes was standing behind it.

"Surprised?" Hayes said with a beaming smile.

Clara blinked, processing.

Maisie spoke before she did. "I'm sure I can speak for all of us when I ask, what is happening right now?"

Hayes laughed then flicked his chin toward Sullivan. "I'm just the helping hand here. Sully better explain."

Sullivan glared at the nickname, but then his expression

softened when his gorgeous eyes met Clara's. "I called in a favor tonight and got you guys a booth for the game."

Again, Clara blinked. "But the other brewery? Won't they—"

"It's fine," Sullivan interjected. "Like I said, I called in a favor, and they don't mind helping out another local brewery trying to push ahead."

Clara felt disoriented. She couldn't believe her eyes or her ears. "So, they just closed for the night?" she asked, trying to understand.

Sullivan shoved his hands into his pockets and gave a sheepish smile. "Well, after I agreed to do a commercial for them."

Time stopped then, and Clara only saw Sullivan there. Raw, trying so damn hard to do right by her.

"Wow," Maisie said after a long moment of silence. "This is...well, totally amazing, Sullivan." She closed the distance and gave him a hug.

Followed up by Amelia. When she stepped back, she added, "The exposure this gives us, it's unbelievable. Thank you so much."

Sullivan smiled like this was everyday business. "You're welcome."

But this wasn't everyday business for Clara. She couldn't take her eyes off him. Not when he watched her with such adoration. Because she knew the truth. He had done this for *her*. To show her he was all in with making her life better. For her. And for Mason. Needing to express her gratitude, she closed the distance and threw her arms around him, holding on tight. He dropped his head into her neck and held her close as the heat of his body enveloped her. "My God, Sullivan, you have gone way above and beyond here."

She leaned away and met the warmth swirling in his eyes. "Thank you for this."

"No thanks needed." He released her, but she got the sense he didn't want to. "I'm glad to do it."

Something passed in the air between them—something that was raw, real, and felt so damn good that Clara never wanted to let go of it.

But, like most things, it didn't last. "While I'm having a blast watching you two hug it out and talk sweet nothings," Hayes commented with laughter in his voice, "we have a lot to do to get ready for tonight. How about we get to it?"

"Right," Sullivan said, stepping away, looking like it was the very last thing he wanted to do.

Amelia studied the booth. "Did you bring enough merchandise?"

Hayes nodded. "I knew the drill and grabbed it all, plus as many kegs that weren't labeled for shipment."

Maisie squeaked a sound of pure happiness then threw herself at him. He kissed her wildly like no one was looking.

Amelia rolled her eyes. "Now who's talking sweet nothings to each other?"

Sullivan chuckled, but Clara couldn't look away from him. Her heart pinged. The way Maisie grabbed Hayes like that, Clara realized she wanted that too. To kiss someone just like that, and she knew exactly who she wanted to kiss too. But then, reality hit. "Mason—"

"I took care of that," Sullivan said with a gentle smile. "Penelope is picking him up after school. She'll bring him home, put him to bed tonight, and will wait for us until we get back."

"You arranged all that?" she asked.

Sullivan cocked his head, his brow wrinkled. "Is that all right? Still not overstepping?"

"No, not at all," Clara said with a disbelieving shake of her head. "More than all right. Sullivan, I'm..." She glanced at her sisters, who wore matching beaming smiles, before adding to him. "I'm not used to having help like this. I don't think I can ever thank you enough."

"Good thing you don't have to thank me, then," Sullivan said. "Better get ready, ladies. Time is counting down." Then he turned and walked away like he wasn't changing their very lives.

With Clara and her sisters busy serving customers from their booth, and having already endured a lecture from his agent about doing a commercial for free, Sullivan headed down the cement staircase toward the visitors' clubhouse. The familiar scents of popcorn and grease followed him on his walk. He'd stayed clear of fans wearing Boston Red Sox's jerseys and baseball caps, keeping his head down, wanting to keep out of sight tonight. The last thing he wanted was the press swarming him for their next hot story. Tonight was all about Clara, and Three Chicks Brewery, and he wanted to keep the focus there. He'd gone past three security checkpoints, but he'd already gotten a pass from security that allowed him through. He felt edgy since he was missing the action. Denver had always been a hard game for him to play, too close to home, but tonight, his edginess was different. He felt different. Above him, fans took their seats, and their loud voices nearly vibrated in the cement hallways.

When he opened the clubhouse's door, he found the team doing what they always did before a game. Some guys were on their phone, a few others were putting golf, and four guys were playing Ping-Pong.

"Keene."

The loud roar of his name came seconds before he was all but jumped by his teammates.

He was tossed around a bit before his good buddy Terrel jabbed him in the gut. "You're looking a little soft, Keene. Have you worked out at all since you've been on suspension?"

Before Sullivan could reply that he'd jogged a little, but not nearly enough, another friend, Jack, yelled, "And we're not talking about skin-to-skin workout."

Sullivan snorted and grinned Jack's way. "Why do you want to know so bad, Lawson? Want a skin-to-skin workout with me?"

More laughter erupted. Sullivan greeted more of the guys, who all asked the same question: when are you coming back? A good question that Sullivan didn't have an answer to. Only one person did. "Where's Coach?" he asked Terrel.

His friend gestured toward a hallway. "In the office." He cupped Sullivan's shoulder. "Good to see you, man."

"Good to be back." Sullivan strode toward the hallway, feeling like as much as he enjoyed being back in River Rock, his heart belonged here too. Baseball had been his savior after his mother passed away. His teammates had been his family when his father turned into a stranger.

He found the coach sitting behind a desk, studying paperwork. Sullivan could only list a half-dozen men who had his respect, but Coach was among them. A family man, he'd played pro ball for twelve years before hanging up his bat to coach. He still looked fit enough to play and worked as hard as anyone on the team. "Coach," he announced.

The coach's head lifted, his Boston Red Sox hat atop his head, covering his clipped salt-and-pepper hair, his brown eyes wide. "Well, damn, Keene, I wasn't expecting to see you tonight."

"I hadn't planned to come," Sullivan said, taking the client chair. "A friend needed a hand."

Coach leaned back in his chair, causing it to squeak beneath him. "Oh, yeah? Do tell."

With the laughter and loud voices of his teammates echoing down the hallway, Sullivan quickly caught the coach up on Clara: who she was to him, his surprise kid, her growing brewery, and everything else in between. The coach knew Sullivan's history. He knew all the pain and heartbreak, every injury his father gave Sullivan, every single tragic detail.

When Sullivan finished, Coach rubbed his jaw. "Damn, Keene, a kid might just be good for you. Kids change you, make you a better man."

Sullivan nodded. "Now, that I believe." He'd only known Mason for a short time, and he felt like he'd already been changed, wanting to do better, be better, not only for himself. For Mason too.

"And this lady of yours, Clara, she sounds like a good woman," Coach said.

"One of the best," Sullivan agreed.

Coach leaned forward, resting his arms on his desk. "You need this in your life, Keene. Stability, it's a good thing. Staying out of the tabloids is even better."

"Yes, sir, we're in full agreement there," Sullivan said.

Someone called the coach's name, which meant the game was about to begin. He rose, approaching Sullivan with his keen eyes. As Sullivan rose as well, Coach stopped in front of him and gave him a look over. "Yeah, I'm liking what I see here. Got a clear head, Keene?"

"I do, sir."

The coach cupped his shoulder, offering a rare smile. "About time, kid. Good to see you're looking so solid. We'll see you when your suspension is up?"

Sullivan nodded. "You will." But as the coach headed off, something about that didn't feel right, either. It occurred to him then that leaving River Rock this time wouldn't be as easy as last time, and last time had nearly killed him.

When the team headed out for the match, and having already been shooed away by all three Carters sisters, Sullivan watched the game next to Hayes. He missed the comradery, the energy from his teammates. He loved the game. Especially as he watched his team win from the sidelines.

By the time the crowds cleared and they made it back upstairs, Sullivan found Clara and her sisters looking exhausted, big smiles on their faces. Popcorn littered the cement floors, alongside spilled beer and plastic cups.

"I take it everything went well?" Sullivan asked, sidling up the booth they'd already begun dismantling.

"So well," Clara said, finishing packing up a box.

"Crazy good," Maisie agreed, as Hayes took over the box she was taping up.

"Oh, my gosh, I think I'm going to fall over," said Amelia, sliding onto her butt in front of the booth.

Sullivan chuckled. It had been a long day. "What can I help with?" he asked.

Clara gestured to the dozen boxes. "All these need to go out."

"On it." Sullivan grabbed what he could, and in no time, the Three Chicks Brewery truck was packed up, and Hayes, Amelia, and Maisie were on the road driving back together. When Sullivan walked toward Clara's car under the beams of the parking lot lights, he asked, "Want me to drive home?"

"Yes, please," she breathed, handing him the keys from her pocket. "Everything on my body hurts right now."

He laughed and wrapped an arm around her waist for support. They'd worked hard tonight. Considering they weren't bringing home any kegs meant they'd sold out.

Once inside the car, Sullivan fastened his seat belt as Clara said, "I don't think you know what today did for us. For days now, I've been stressing if I had enough leverage to ask for more demands in our contracts." She glanced his way, expression soft and warm. "Without any doubt in my mind, you got us that today. You did more than any distributor could do for us, and you did all that without asking for a thing."

His chest expanded to its fullest as he spotted the Clara he had always loved in the depths of her eyes. Feeling like nothing lay between them, he said, "Whatever I can do to help you, Clara, I will."

The lights from the dashboard lit up her face as her eyes searched his. "Why are you doing all this?"

Only the truth would keep them moving forward. "To gain your forgiveness. To earn your trust."

Emotion filled her eyes as she leaned in closer then, the air heating up between them in the car. "You don't have to keep doing these amazing things for me."

"Yeah, I do," he said then cupped her warm cheek, heat flooding his groin at her nearness. "Because you did amazing things for me too, including raising our son when I wasn't well enough to." He brushed the softness of her cheek, lost in the way she watched him so eagerly. "So, yes, Clara, I do need to do these things. It's about time someone looked after you like you've looked after others."

Her soft smile was his greatest reward.

Captivated by her, he dropped his mouth to hers, and he let himself enjoy the slow kiss, not allowing it to heat up, not building desire, simply giving them this moment. And there, in the sweetness of her embrace, he found something bigger than himself or his past; he found another purpose than baseball. Making Clara happy and taking care of her felt as good as any home run he'd ever hit out of the park.

When she leaned away, she said with a laugh, "I hope you don't expect more than a kiss, because my body is not capable of even moving right now."

He reached across her and fastened her seat belt. "I expect you to sleep while I get us home safe."

"Thank goodness." She yawned and shut her eyes but reached for his hand first, twining her delicate fingers with his.

Soon, they were on their way, leaving the city behind for the quiet country roads, and for the first time ever, he realized his suspension was the greatest thing to have ever have happened to him. Because it had brought him back to her.

10

"So, you have a son," the chief stated, sitting across from Sullivan a week later in the hotspot restaurant in downtown, The Kitchen. The space was as fancy as any place in Boston with its wooden beams on the ceiling, dark stone on the walls, and sleek metal tables. Every table and booth was occupied, a telling sign the food was top-notch. The aroma in the air was a mix of freshly brewed coffee and perfectly cooked bacon, but the company was better. For the last half an hour, Sullivan had caught John up on the bar fight, the suspension, the reason he came home, and now, the most wonderful surprise of all, Mason. This great kid that radiated happiness and reminded Sullivan of his once-happy childhood.

"That must have been a surprise," John stated when Sullivan finished.

"That's putting it lightly," Sullivan said, cutting into his over-easy egg with his fork. "But it's a good surprise, and I think that surprises me most of all." Years back, before everything went to shit, Sullivan had wanted to be a family man. A good father, unlike his own, but that dream had faded.

John studied Sullivan over the rim of his cup before he took a sip of his coffee. "I asked Hayes once if Mason was yours. He looks like your mother."

Sullivan agreed with a nod. "He's got her eyes."

"Yup, that's what I thought too." John reached for his toast. "I take it Clara had a good reason to keep such a big secret." He took a bite.

"Just protecting him," Sullivan said, knowing he wouldn't need to say more. John knew every aspect of Sullivan's life, more than anyone else since he had worked his case. He'd seen every bruise, every stitch.

Once John swallowed his toast, he wiped his mouth with his napkin. "Listen, Sullivan, you know I've never been good at beating around the bush, so let's get to it." He leaned forward, setting his arms beside his plate. "You're a damn good ballplayer. Your mother would be immensely proud of all that you've accomplished, but there is more to life than playing ball. It looks like you're finally seeing that. You've got far more of your mother's loving nature in you than your father's hot temper, and you'll make an incredible father to Mason. Just have to get out of your head and believe it, is all."

Sullivan snorted a laugh. "That simple, huh?"

"Life typically is that simple when you are your worst enemy," John said.

"I suppose that's true," Sullivan agreed. John had been the solid ground in Sullivan's life when he needed that. He'd been the shoulder to lean on and the listener when he needed that too. "You know, I never thanked you for what you did for me."

John set the fork he'd picked up back down. "You never

needed to thank me, Sullivan. Nothing makes me happier than seeing you doing well." And obviously done with getting the thank you he deserved, he said, "Now let's talk sports."

By the time they parted ways, Sullivan's head swarmed with thoughts. The plan had always been to come home, face the shit he'd been running from, and get his head together. But he was more confused than ever. Because what he'd been running from, now looked perfect, and he didn't want to leave. He had friends in River Rock, chosen family. He had Clara and Mason. So, when Sullivan arrived for his therapy appointment, he suspected the doctor would see right through him.

Elizabeth looked as buttoned-up as always. She sat across from him, light spilling in from the window off to her right. "Let's talk about your suspension. Has this happened before?"

He shook his head. "The press follows me more now. It's not an ideal situation since my actions are caught on camera. That's all this was. A few too many drinks met with an arrogant prick who pushed his girlfriend and deserved a shot in the face."

Elizabeth made a note then raised her brows at him. "It doesn't sound like you deserved a suspension for that."

He leaned back in the comfortable couch, crossing his ankle over his knee. "Sometimes, it's easier to take the punishment than deal with a long, drawn-out investigation. They had me on tape, hitting the guy. The coach recommended I take the month off. I'd stirred up enough shit that I just took the suspension."

She made another note. "Why is the press following you more now?"

He noted how she asked questions without judgment,

and he liked it. "I had a good year playing, matched with a couple high-profile women in my life." One was an actress. The other a singer. "Apparently, I'm good for gaining readership on social media, so they've upped their invasion of my life."

"I did read an article after the altercation," Elizabeth said. "It didn't paint you in the best light."

"Of course it didn't," Sullivan countered. "Rags never do. But the damage was done, and the coach couldn't overlook it, nor could the owner of the team. I'm a role model for kids, whether I like it or not, and I displayed bad sportsman-like behavior."

She made another note before looking back up at him. "You didn't mind the punishment, then?"

"Of course I minded it," he countered. "But I understood it. They had to make an example of me. I didn't realize the paparazzi had gotten so close. Now I know. It won't happen again. Besides, things are different now."

"Why is that?"

He paused to consider how he should explain this. "I found out I have a son."

She froze, statue-still. "Here, in River Rock?"

He nodded then answered her unasked questions. "No, I didn't know about him, and no, I'm not upset my ex didn't tell me. I walked out on her, a complete mess of a man, and didn't answer her call when she tried to tell me about our son. If I were in her spot, I would have done the same damn thing. She protected her child; I won't ever fault her for that."

Elizabeth studied him. Sullivan got the impression his response surprised her.

"So, you have a son," she eventually said. "That must have been quite a shock."

"Definitely," Sullivan admitted. "But it's a good shock. He's a cool kid."

Elizabeth made another note, and Sullivan would have paid a lot of money to read that paper as Elizabeth asked, "Does your son know you're his father?"

"Yes, we told him last week."

She looked up from her notepad. "You and your ex told him?"

"That's right."

Elizabeth set her pen down on the notepad. "So, you and your son's mother are talking again?"

He nodded, and seeing that he didn't feel the need to hide anything, he added, "Among other things."

Elizabeth remained stone-faced. She uncrossed her legs then crossed them again, regarding Sullivan intently. "Just so I have all the facts: you've reunited with the woman you say you left behind, only to find out you have a son you didn't know about. This is a lot for anyone, Sullivan. How are you feeling about all this?"

Good. Amazing. Happy. But considering the tension on Elizabeth's face, he figured that was the wrong answer. "How should I be feeling about this?" he asked.

She responded with a soft smile. "That's not for me to answer, Sullivan."

His chest squeezed. He tried to sort through all he felt, but it seemed impossible. He looked to her window, where a tree danced in the wind. "I'm not sure I need to feel anything. It is what it is. We can only move forward now, and everyone seems happy."

"Interesting perspective," Elizabeth said.

Sullivan's gaze snapped to her, his chest heating under the firmness in her eyes. "But you think it's wrong?"

"No perspective is wrong," Elizabeth countered gently.

"But I would ask you: how is that perspective working for you in your life?"

His lips parted to say everything was fine and things were good, but he shut his mouth tight. For nearly seven years, he'd been running from his choice to leave River Rock behind. He'd taken women to his bed to forget the one woman who held his heart. Now he was back, and while he felt like he and Clara were healing, he still had a lot to face. "I'd say that perhaps my perspective needs some tweaking."

Elizabeth gave a gentle nod. "If I could offer you some advice, I would say this: you need to go back, Sullivan, revisit the pivotal moments that shaped your life up until this point and face them. Not only for yourself, but for your son." *And for the mother of your child,* she didn't say aloud, but he heard anyway. She set her paper down on the table. "You're with me because something in your life isn't working and it's leading you on a path that's hurting you. But to work on that, you need to face the things that put you on this path in the first place. There are no shortcuts."

He glanced away to the window again, swallowing hard. "I can't face the reason I left River Rock. Both of them are dead."

"Here on Earth," she said so softly, drawing Sullivan's gaze again. She placed a hand on her chest. "But not here." She tapped her chest once more. "Here, they are never dead."

Sullivan felt the ground shake beneath him. He rose, moved to the window, and stared out, wishing he could get in a big gulp of fresh air. "So, what are you suggesting here? I go and chat it out with my parents in the cemetery?"

"If that would help, then, yes," Elizabeth said, matter-of-factly from behind him. "I'm not here to give you the answers, Sullivan. I'm here to help guide you. Your life is yours. The time we've had together is all we've got. Have you done everything you came here to do?"

He glanced over his shoulder. "And what if I haven't?"

Her smile became all too knowing. "Then, you owe it to yourself to find peace. If you feel you've got what you needed out of our sessions then great, but—"

"You think I haven't?"

Again, she gave a polite smile. "I think you've shown up. But you're edgy. I can see you're looking for peace, Sullivan, and to find that, you need to put in the work. You need to face things you don't want to face. And ask hard questions."

He arched an eyebrow. "What questions?"

"Why did you run from a woman you obviously loved? Why has it taken you seven years to come home?" She hesitated like she knew those questions were like knives to Sullivan's gut. "Go back to the place where you hit a dead end and your life forked in a new direction. See what you find there."

Sullivan looked back out the window, watching the leaves flickering on the branches. He knew exactly where he needed to go to find that fork in his life. The one place he hadn't been since he was twenty-one years old.

Home.

The gloomy, rainy morning had come and gone, and Clara had finished up lunch and put her dirty dishes in the dishwasher when there was a knock at the door. With Amelia busy in the brewery, Clara hurried to answer, expecting a delivery. However, when she opened the door, she found Sullivan, looking...different. There was a stillness about him that she'd never seen before as rain battered the ground. "Is everything okay?" she asked, opening the door wider.

He gave a small nod. "I know you're working, but could you take some time away and come with me somewhere?"

She glanced at her watch. *12:32.* "I've got an hour or so before I've got a meeting scheduled with our lawyer to finalize the contracts."

"I'll get you back before it starts," he promised.

Lost in the tense set of his eyes, she recognized that dark pain. "Should I be worried?"

"No, I'm all right," he said, twining his warm fingers with hers, holding strong. "Truly. I just want you with me."

Her heart flipped, overexposing all the soft spots to him, and she went with him without further thought. Curious, but letting him think through whatever was on his mind, she stayed silent next to him on the drive as the windshield wipers worked to clear the sheet of rain off the windshield. Until she realized he was heading to the one place she thought he'd never go: his childhood home. The light blue two-story house with the simple perennial gardens. "Have you been by here yet?" she asked, wondering why he'd come here.

He shook his head, put the truck in park, and turned it off, emotion filling his eyes.

The street was quiet, save for one man walking his dog down the other side of the road with an umbrella and a rain jacket on the dog. For Clara, Good memories lived on this street, and she assumed for Sullivan too, until those memories faded into all the bad ones.

A beat passed. "Did you talk to your dad after you left?" she asked, breaking the silence, needing to hear his thoughts.

"No," he said, with no hint of remorse in his voice.

"When I left, I left him behind." He studied the house, running a hand through his hair. "I'm surprised the house is still standing. I figured someone would have knocked it down and rebuilt it."

"Well...it's still standing because your dad left it to me." Sullivan's head whirled so fast toward Clara, she laughed softly. "You never knew?"

"No. Never," he stated, shaking his head slowly. "But I also never returned the lawyer's phone calls or letters when he contacted me. I had my agent, Marco, tell him to donate whatever money my father had to a cancer charity. I signed the necessary documents, and that was that." He paused, his eyes searching hers. "Why would he leave you—"

She could see the exact moment when he realized why, and she nodded. "It's complicated. He knew Mason was yours, but I'm not sure that's the only reason he left me the house."

"Did you tell him?"

She let out a long breath, leaning her head back against the headrest before answering. "After that day I confronted him, I didn't see your dad for a while." She looked out at the house she'd had painted last year by some students looking for work. She'd had a kid down the road cut the grass, and she tended to the gardens when she could. But the house had remained empty because Clara had no idea what to do with it. "But after a while, I heard he'd lost a lot of weight and was doing really bad, so I brought him food once a week and left it on the porch."

When she looked back at Sullivan, his expression went blank, revealing nothing. "Why would you show him that kindness after what he did?"

Back then, she'd questioned her sanity too. "It's hard to explain. It's not like I liked him. I didn't. Actually, back then,

I hated him for what he did to you. But..." She looked out at the house, and her heart ached, remembering that time. "But I guess a part of me understood him. I knew how it felt to have someone you love ripped from your life." She felt every bit of the silence and turned back to Sullivan to explain. "I'm not saying I thought he wasn't a horrible person for doing what he did to you, but I couldn't leave him to..." She paused again and then shrugged. "I just couldn't let him rot in this house. I wanted..."

"To remind him that someone cared."

"I guess something like that," she agreed with a nod. "And he was, and always would be, Mason's grandfather."

Sullivan watched her closely, his expression closed off while a hundred things likely played through his mind. Finally, he glanced down at his hands, head bowed. "He didn't deserve your kindness, but he was lucky to have it. He never came out when you dropped off the food? Never talked to you?"

"No."

Sullivan's head lifted, his gaze raw with pain. "Then, how did he know about Mason?"

Clara recalled that day and inhaled against the swell of emotion squeezing her throat. "I was picking up wine at the store. Mason was only three then. But we were going in, and your father was coming out. I almost didn't recognize him."

"He looked like a drunk?"

"Worse than drunk," Clara explained. "He looked dead." She shut her eyes, wishing she could forget that day. "I'd never seen anyone look like that before. When he saw me, he froze, and I could tell he wanted to say something. Maybe even thank me for the food."

Beside her, Sullivan's voice was soft. "Did he thank you?"

She swallowed the hard lump in her throat and looked

Sullivan's way again, finding his expression full of longing. "I think he almost did, but he looked down at Mason, and it was like he'd seen a ghost. I didn't have to say anything. Your dad knew right then who Mason was."

Sullivan rubbed the back of his corded neck. "What happened then?"

Clara remembered this part with a smile. "Mason, being Mason, stuck out his hand and said, '*Hello, I'm Mason Carter.*' Your father didn't say anything, but he did shake Mason's hand. I thought that was it, but right before he walked away, he looked at me and said, '*You are my sun, my moon, and all my stars.*'"

"Jesus," Sullivan breathed. He thrust his hands into his hair and dropped his head, a slight tremble rolling through him.

Emotion rippled across Sullivan's face, and Clara felt each one of those emotions deep in her core too. "I take it that means something to you?"

Sullivan glanced her way, and his voice shook. "It's a quote my mom used to always say to me."

Tears filled Clara's eyes as Sullivan became blurry next to her. She reached for him, needing to get closer, squeezing his hand tightly. "My God, Sullivan."

Sullivan blew out a long breath, tipping his head back. "Maybe he wasn't all the way gone."

"Not that day," she said, placing her other hand over the top of his, and repeated, "Not that day."

A long moment settled between them. The rain continued its rhythmic taps against the windshield. Sullivan watched her, and she watched him right back. It occurred to her she was there for one important reason—to remind him he wasn't alone. So, she kept silent, letting his soul recover from the damaging memories that had haunted him for years.

Until Sullivan broke the silence. "I want to do better. I want to do right by Mason. And by you."

Knowing he needed to let all this go to move forward, she cupped his face. "You can't change the past, Sullivan. What's done is done, but you can choose a better future, where you forgive what's happened and find peace."

His gaze held hers, a thousand things being said between them without anything being said at all. "I thought moving away would fix everything for everybody." His eyes skipped past Clara and landed back on the house. "But this house, the damage done here, I was running from it. And I've never been able to stop running." When he looked at Clara again, there was strength and resolve in the depths of his eyes. He leaned closer and took her chin in his grip. "How can I ever repay you? I'd like to say thank you for everything you have done, but I'm not sure that's enough. Or will ever be enough."

"It's enough, Sullivan." She threw her arms around him, holding him tight, feeling the last strands of what stood between them break apart. "It will always be enough."

11

That Saturday evening, Sullivan felt a shift in his chest, a connection to life, growing in a way he'd never experienced before or expected. Surrounded by the Colorado mountains, with their snowy peaks, he clicked his tongue, sending the horse beneath him cantering forward. He was at Beckett's workplace, Blackshaw Cattle Farm and Guest Ranch. He'd learned earlier from Mason that family rides were something Clara and Mason did together often, and the Blackshaw family had some good horses they could rent to ride. Ahead of him, Clara and her sisters rode Quarter Horses while Mason was atop a Pinto pony, a black cowboy hat on his head, and Hayes was next to Maisie on a dapple gray stallion. The sun would set within a half hour, and the Colorado sky was showing off with its warm orange and purple hues. When Sullivan got closer to the group, he called to his horse, "Whoa." The chestnut gelding slowed to a walk next to Beckett.

"Was wondering when we were finally going to get you

out for a ride," Beckett said with a smirk, riding atop a stunning roan mare.

"I'm sure I'll feel this tomorrow," Sullivan said, adjusting the reins in his left hand. "It's been a long time."

Beckett smirked then gestured ahead. "Things are going well, I see."

"Better than I hoped," Sullivan admitted, settling into the quietness around him and the swishing of the long grass against his horse's leg as they ventured farther into the meadow. "Want to tell me what happened there?" he asked, gesturing toward the woman Beckett couldn't take his eyes off.

His friend blinked and looked Sullivan's way. "Amelia is engaged to someone else. Isn't it pretty clear what happened?"

Sullivan gave an easy shrug. "Probably to some, but I remember our talks about her." Beckett had been smitten, and he'd done nothing to hide that fact.

The corner of Beckett's eyes tightened as his gaze returned to Amelia again. "She wanted to see what the world had to offer, so she went to the big city, and I let her go, thinking she'd come back to me."

"But she didn't?"

Beckett snorted. "She came back with an idiot for a fiancé."

Sullivan considered what he'd heard as his horse set a steady pace across the meadow. The scent of warm earth and sunlight became all-consuming. Mason kept trotting ahead, and he'd hear Clara yell after him. The kid was a good cowboy, and Sullivan wondered if that was his future path. "So, that's where you left things, then?" Sullivan asked, turning his focus back onto Beckett.

Beckett's gaze slid Sullivan's way, and he nodded. "She's happy. Who am I to get in the way of that?"

"Fair point," Sullivan hedged. "What happens if she's ever not happy?"

Beckett's grin turned wicked and determined. "Then, she'll be mine again." With a click of his tongue, his horse shot forward at a gallop and then slowed as he settled in next to Amelia, who gave him a smile filled with warmth.

Yeah, maybe they weren't done just yet.

"Mason, that's too far ahead," Clara yelled. *Again.*

Sullivan squeezed his feet, and his horse broke into a floaty lope, reaching Mason quickly. "Where are you off to?" Sullivan asked.

Mason kicked the pony's sides, frowning. "He won't go faster." The pony practically snarled and gave a little buck.

Sullivan laughed as it jolted Mason out of the saddle. "That's probably a good thing. Go on over with your aunts, buddy. Need to stay close, all right?"

"Fine," Mason said, pulling on his rein and giving the pony another kick. The fat animal barely trotted back to the group.

Sullivan made a kissing noise, and his horse shot forward until he slowed him again, settling in next to Clara.

"Thank you for that," she said with a sweet smile from atop her horse. "Sometimes he forgets horseback riding can be dangerous."

Sullivan smiled back. "Maybe he needs something that moves faster than a turtle." When Clara laughed, he added, "He's a good little cowboy. Is there anything he can't do?"

She gave a knowing look. "He's athletic. I wonder who he gets that from."

Sullivan chuckled with her, rested his hand holding the reins on the horn of the saddle, and breathed in the fresh air. Birds sang and chirped in every direction as shafts of the golden sun lit up the meadow in patches. The others were well ahead of him, and after hearing Mason was athletic and taking the private moment, he said, "We haven't discussed all this yet, but sports and everything else are expensive, and I owe you child support."

She shook her head, adamant. "You don't need—"

"I do. I need to," he countered.

The sun hit her face just right, bringing out the red hues in her hair. She watched him closely then offered, "All right, then let's do this; we'll get in contact with a lawyer and see how much you would have paid. Whatever that amount is, let's put it into a savings account for him for college. Is that fair?"

"Yes," he agreed. "Makes sense."

She smiled and exhaled, tipping her head back and soaking up the last couple of hours of daylight. She'd never looked more beautiful as she continued, "We can talk later about financial help going forward once we get everything else figured out."

He understood. A lot hung in the balance.

She glanced his way again and added, "I think the biggest thing to work out is the logistics. I mean, are you even set up for him to visit you in Boston?"

"I've got a condo." The space was set up for a busy bachelor. He had no backyard. No play gym. "It's not exactly kid-friendly, but I can move."

"Really?" she asked, brows lifted. "You're going to move, just like that?"

"Without a doubt," he said, adamant. "I'll do what Mason needs."

Slight hesitation crossed her face, erasing the gentle peace he'd witnessed a moment ago. "While I appreciate everything you're doing and plan to do going forward, I know this is a lot. Mason changed my life in huge ways when he came into the picture, and I had months to get ready for him. I can only imagine how jarring this all is." She stopped her horse, and he pulled on his reins too as she added, "So, I want you to understand that it's okay if we take two steps forward, one step back. We don't need to rush anything. We need to let Mason get to know you, and you get to know him. For now, when you go back to Boston, we can FaceTime or Zoom. Maybe I can fly out with him and we can come to a game. Once the season is over, you can find a place and get settled. And if Mason wants to, he can come out for a visit. Okay?"

Yeah, he liked that idea, but... "What if I decide not to leave River Rock?"

"That's silly," she said with a snort. "What are you going to do, retire from baseball?"

"It is one option," he told her.

She rolled her eyes as her horse started walking again. "Again, that's silly."

His horse quickly caught up. "Why is it silly?"

A big cloud drifted overhead, shadowing Clara as she said, "Because playing baseball is your dream, and you're damn good at it."

He considered, and the thought of leaving baseball gutted him. But at the same time, things had changed. He didn't feel like the guy he'd been before the suspension. "But dreams change, people change."

"Don't do that," she snapped, stopping her horse once more. Her firm gaze met his. "The greatest thing you could ever teach Mason is that living your passion and following your dreams is important. We can make this work. Sure, it might take a little wrangling to figure out the logistics, but please, don't for one second think I would want you to walk away from baseball. In fact, that would break my heart. Baseball is in your soul. You retire when you're ready, not because of us. I won't have that. All right?"

Damn, he loved when she told things straight. It reminded him she wasn't a young twenty-one-year-old woman anymore. She was twenty-eight and had her shit together. He liked that. Hell, he respected and envied that. "All right," he said, before watching as she trotted off toward Mason.

Sullivan's gaze fell to Amelia and Beckett, and seeing his friend's longing for her made things very clear. He didn't want to be longing for Clara. He wanted to be *with* Clara. He'd made the mistakes in the past, but then and there, he promised himself that he wouldn't make the same mistakes again.

Long after the ride was over, and with Mason tucked away in bed and sound asleep, Clara stripped off her clothes, tossing them into the laundry hamper in the closet. Amelia had decided to go into the city for the night and was sleeping over at Luka's, so Clara embraced a side of herself that rarely came out to play. She turned the mama-mode switch off and settled into the naked skin of a woman needing some hot pleasure. She clicked the lock on her bedroom closed and then turned her attention to the shower, where Sullivan was washing off from the long ride. Heat and desire flooded her as she moved into the bath-room, her nipples puckering in anticipation. Years back, she'd been more reserved, shy. She wasn't that twenty-one-year-old woman anymore. She knew what she wanted, and the gorgeous sculpted-to-pure-perfection man behind the shower curtain was exactly who she wanted. "Sullivan," she called, not wanting to scare him.

"Be done in a minute," he answered.

Yeah, not good enough for her. She pulled the shower curtain aside and got a good look at Sullivan Keene soaking wet, partly covered in soap. His muscular physique was in tip-top shape, his skin a gorgeous golden, and an impressively thick cock was growing harder with every second that he watched her.

He made a low noise in the back of his throat, scanning over her naked flesh. Then he arched an eyebrow. "Well, now, that's the look of a woman who wants something."

"I'll start with your mouth," she said, climbing into the shower and closing the curtain behind her.

He grinned, his damp hair falling over his brow. "Bossy, huh?"

"Not bossy," she corrected. "Horny."

His gaze roamed over her parted lips before his heated stare returned to hers. "Best I see to that, then." He slid an arm around her and pulling her under the shower's head. His gaze followed the water sliding down her chest, and he slid his hand lower against the small of her back, pulling her up against his erection.

She moaned her response. Passion and lust burned between them as his lips met hers and his kiss took her far away from there. Desperation overwhelmed her as she dragged her hands over his strong shoulders and down his biceps. Soon, he turned her around, her back to his chest. His hands explored her breasts, massaging, squeezing, tweaking her nipples, while his mouth continued to play on her neck. She wiggled against him, needing him, overwhelmed by the strength of him.

Hot and done with teasing, she turned around and pushed a little, sending him walking backward. His thick cock became her whole focus, and she indulged herself, lowering to her knees, never taking her eyes off his.

Hungry eyes met hers as he dragged his thumb across her lips, arching an eyebrow. "I thought you wanted my mouth, Slugger?"

"I've changed my mind," she said, running her fingers up his smooth six-pack until she wrapped her hand around the hard length of him. His low groan rippled across her. "I want this so much more." Desperate to taste him, to see his gaze smolder from the pleasure she gave, she took him deep into her mouth. With the warm water splashing around them, she licked and swirled and played with him until she felt his legs tremble, saw the hunger deepen in his expression, and heard his rough growl. Only then did she close her eyes, focusing entirely on his pleasure, stroking him until his groans vibrated through her.

She felt him stiffen, nearly finish, but then she was in his arms. He turned off the shower and carried her to the bed, and she bounced on the mattress as he laid her out. He grinned wickedly—a smile that damn near stopped her heart—as he slid between her thighs.

"You're not allowed to have all the fun." At the first contact of his tongue against her needy flesh, she grabbed a fistful of bedsheets and arched up into the pleasure. His tongue was gentle and wet and warm, and each teasingly light stroke made her want more. *Need* more.

Reading her just right, his finger slid over her clit and stroked in lazy circles before gingerly moving down her folds until he entered her. She moaned greedily, shifting her hips against him and riding his fingers, desperate for *more*.

"Don't worry, Slugger," he said, pressing a soft kiss against her inner thigh. "I'll get you there."

Her heady moan was her only reply.

One finger soon became two, and those teasingly light strokes of his tongue heightening her pleasure, turning it into something else entirely. His fingers pumped now, his mouth sucking and flicking, and she moaned and wiggled into the pleasure, kept in place only by his arm pinning her. Building and building, until all that pleasure stormed in, taking her far away from there.

She vaguely remembered him flipping her onto her knees that barely supported her before she felt the latex between them. But then she became lost as he entered her and moved slowly at first. He pressed against her back, sending her bottom into the air. His dominating fingers gripped her hips, and she pushed back against him. She felt all of him and knew he felt all of her too. Soon, he began rocking into her. Hard. Fast. He gave no misunderstanding that he was wild for her. As he pounded into her, she hung on for the ride. And it was a great fucking ride.

His hands were everywhere, stroking, seducing, commanding her. Somewhere in the pleasure, a new sensation rose, one she grabbed onto and never wanted to let go. Here, in the strength of his arms, she let go. Completely. His strength became all-consuming, and she melted into his addictive pleasure.

Then he went even harder. Skin slapping rhythmically against skin. The scent of their sex filling her senses. It became too much—so good she couldn't hold onto it anymore.

She came first, with her scream muffled in the pillow and her toes curled from the pleasure, and he followed behind with a strained groan. They fell apart together, tangled into each other, and she settled into the crook of his shoulder, both of them breathless and sweaty. She shut her eyes and let her mind relax, wondering if she could bottle up a moment and keep it forever. Because if she could, she would pick this moment, this quietness sliding over her. This peace and happiness.

Sullivan finally broke the silence. "I could get used to this."

"Cuddling?" Clara asked with a laugh.

"Yes," he said, seriously, stroking his fingers through her hair.

She leaned up to look at him, finding his eyes closed, a peaceful expression on his face. "You haven't cuddled in a while?"

He peeked open an eye and gave a soft smile. "No, not like this."

Her heart nearly jumped out of her chest, and she smiled in return. "Well, you're not alone there. I can't remember the last time I cuddled with anyone." Yeah, she could. It had happened seven years ago, with *him*.

He continued to stroke her hair. "You were never serious with anyone after me?"

"No," she answered before she wondered if maybe she shouldn't have.

His reply came just as quickly, settling her worries. "Me neither."

The loaded statement hung in the air between them, and Clara felt his arm tightening around her. "It's not like I didn't want to find anything serious," she explained. "I just didn't have the time for it."

His hand froze. "Was there anyone at all?"

"Of course, just nothing serious. I had my fun when I could, but kept things casual. Just made things easier where it came to Mason. What about you? Were the tabloids always wrong about your love life?"

"In that regard, they were always right," he muttered sleepily. "And like I told you before, for me, women were a distraction, an escape. I never made any promises."

A long moment passed between them, a thousand unsaid things spiraling in the air between them. Until one thought stood out that she couldn't push away. "Do you think that's weird?" Clara asked, putting a voice to her worries. "That neither of us really moved on?"

"No." He slid over her until he hovered above her, his damp hair curtaining his face. "And you know why?"

She became lost in his steady gaze as she slid her hands over his strong shoulders, down his flexed biceps, feeling him shiver under her touch. "Why?"

He dropped his mouth to hers. "Because we weren't done yet."

"No, I guess we weren't," she whispered against his lips, and then she let him claim her again.

12

Two weeks went in a blur of magic and possibilities, and Clara knew with each passing day that she was letting herself fall deeper for Sullivan. Everything was perfect, and during the time she had with him, she felt like she finally had the family she wanted, with Sullivan in their lives. He'd done the work, on himself and for her and Mason. She woke up this morning, and like she did every other day, she got Mason off to school before returning home to work. Only today, everything felt different, she felt...*hopeful*. Mason was happy and thriving, and Sullivan was fitting into their lives seamlessly. And while it still felt like they needed to go slowly, she knew she wanted to take these steps forward with Sullivan. Lately, everything seemed perfect, so perfect that she wondered if maybe, *just maybe*, this time everything would be different. That this time, they would get their forever they had once talked about.

With the exposure from Sullivan's media stunt at the brewery and the baseball game lighting up their social media and causing their beer to sell out locally, Clara decided to send her final revisions of the contracts back to her lawyer for him to send off to the distributors for final negotiations. The terms were much better for the brewery mainly due to Sullivan's help. So she grabbed a coffee from the coffee shop and returned home to get this deal done.

For once in a very long time, Clara let her heart bask in the happy glow. The day was clear without a cloud in the sky. The roads were quiet. And even though gossip had spread about Mason being Sullivan's son after Mason told everyone at school, the townsfolk had been kind and understanding, not catty. Everything was perfect.

Until she arrived home and all hell broke loose.

Before Clara could even park, people swarmed her car. No, not people, she realized: reporters. A dozen in total, some with cameras, others with microphones, and some with video cameras. She exited the car, looking for Sullivan somewhere in the crowd, but he was nowhere in sight. "Excuse me. Please, excuse me," she said, pushing through the people, feeling like a sardine in a can.

"Clara. Clara," a reporter called. "Please, over here, Clara."

A blink of the eye later, she found microphones shoved in her face, the flash of cameras blinding her, questions being hurled her way. Their voices blended together in a roar, making it impossible for her to make out what they were saying.

Feeling trapped and claustrophobic, she wiggled out from around them and ran toward the house, not looking back. Just as she made it to the porch, she spotted Sullivan running toward her from his rental truck.

He met her halfway, his eyes hard, angry. "Go inside. Now. Call the police."

She didn't need him to ask her twice. She booked it forward, running up the porch steps, and got inside in a second flat, slamming the door shut behind her. Her purse fell to the hardwood floor, and she dropped to her knees, ignoring the sharp pain and grabbing her phone out with shaky hands. "Hello, this is Clara Carter, over at Three Chicks Brewery," she said, breathless. "I've just arrived home to a dozen of unwanted reporters on my property." In hopes they'd get here fast, she added, "They're being forceful in their questioning."

A pause. Then the 911 operator said, "We'll send a few cruisers out to the brewery now. Hang tight."

"Thank you," Clara breathed, ending the call. One of the blessings of living in a small town was not having to explain more than she had to nor give an address. She stayed right there, in the foyer, with her cell phone clenched in her hand, and breathed past the shakiness, trembling to her core.

After a moment, Amelia ran from the kitchen and snapped, "Thank goodness you're home. I've been calling, but you must have had your phone on silent. I had no idea what to do. Do you know why they're here?"

"I haven't got a clue." Feeling like her legs were under her again, Clara rose and moved into the living room. She pulled the flower-patterned curtain aside to sneak a look outside. Sullivan stood at the bottom of the porch steps, talking to the reporters still yelling out to him. "It's a madhouse out there. I've never seen anything like that."

Amelia peeked around the curtain too. "Do you think that's all for Sullivan?"

"Maybe because his suspension is ending soon. Who knows?" Her heart went out to him. Is this what he faced all the time? Where was the privacy?

"Sorry to break it to you, but it has nothing to do with his suspension."

Clara whirled around to Maisie. "Then, what is it about?" she demanded.

Maisie cringed. "Fair warning: you're not going to like what I'm about to show you."

Clara noted Maisie's shoes were still on, indicating she'd come through the back door. It didn't take much to know something was terribly wrong. One look at Maisie's curled shoulders said enough. "Consider me warned. What is it?" Clara asked.

Maisie's brow wrinkled as she closed the distance to offer her cell phone. "I saw this in my news feed on Facebook. I came right away."

First, Clara made out she was looking at an article from a trashy rag. Then she stopped breathing at the headline: SULLIVAN KEENE HAS A SECRET LOVE CHILD. That in itself wasn't the only problem; it was all the details of their lives that followed. They'd twisted every event that shaped their lives. They knew he'd left her, and they blamed him. Only him. And the final sentence in the article was a dagger to her heart: CAN SHE FORGIVE HIM FOR WALKING OUT ON HER SON AND HER?

"Oh, my God," Clara breathed, glancing up at Maisie. "How could they do this to Sullivan? To Mason?" Word after word, it painted them in the worst light. Sullivan looked no better than his abusive father. Clara looked like a weak woman who drowned without Sullivan, barely able to raise her son. Mason was dragged through the mud alongside her and Sullivan. "How could they do this to a child?"

Maisie recoiled. "I know. It's bad. I'm sorry, Clara."

Amelia scooped up the phone, read the article, and growled, "And why do they care anyway if he left and moved away? Or that you have a son together? Don't they have more important news to report on instead of Sullivan's personal life?"

Clara had seen Sullivan's face on the grocery store tabloids for years. "Not when Sullivan sells magazines." The worst part was that the picture they had used was from when they went to the zoo together. A reporter had obviously been following them. They'd taken a happy moment and twisted it until it became ugly. The photograph was of Mason running away from them, and while they hadn't been arguing at all, Sullivan had his head bowed and looked sad. Clara remembered that moment. Sullivan had wanted to tell Mason the truth and not keep secrets anymore. "Why would they do this to him?" she asked, mostly to herself, shaking her head.

"Because they're paparazzi," Maisie said, peeking around the curtain and out the window. "They're paid to twist stories."

Amelia handed Maisie her phone back then said to Clara, "This doesn't matter. They don't matter. Anyone who believes this trash talk doesn't matter."

But someone did matter, someone above anyone else. "Mason matters." Clara took the phone from Maisie again, searching for anything bad said about Mason. While he wasn't mentioned directly, the article stated that Clara hated Sullivan for leaving them, and that Sullivan hadn't wanted a son. Her heart squeezed tight. Gossip ran like wildfire through town, which was likely how the reporters got wind of Sullivan's son no one knew about. Surely, a kid a school would mention it to Mason and bully him. Especially since Mason had been boasting about his dad being a professional baseball player. She never wanted Mason to think Sullivan didn't want him.

With trembling limbs, she moved back to the window, watching Sullivan talking to the reporters, handling them like he seemed to do so well. But she wasn't used to any of this, and her head swarmed with worries. "This is our story, not theirs, and they've twisted it. Made it so ugly."

Before Clara could even think what to do next, the front door opened, and Hayes rushed in. "Fucking vultures," he growled.

But in that exact moment, before Hayes slammed the door shut, Clara heard something else.

"Do you still love Clara Carter?" a reporter called. "Did you ever love her?"

It occurred to her right then that she had been fooling herself. And that, from day one when it came to Sullivan, she'd been all in. Because her unguarded heart bled as Sullivan answered, "No, not now. Not ever."

13

An hour had gone by since the cops showed up at the brewery to clear out the reporters, and Sullivan's mood was in no better state than when he'd arrived after being alerted to the article by Marco. "Thank you for coming by," Sullivan said to Penelope's husband and cop, Darryl, as the sun sank lower behind the mountains.

Standing on the porch steps, Darryl rested his hand on the barrel of his weapon. He was a scruffy guy with a thick beard, tough for sure. "Hey, man, not a problem. Sorry you're dealing with this. Let me know if you need me to come back."

"Thanks," Sullivan said, his jaw muscles clenching and unclenching against the frustration burning through him.

As Darryl headed down the porch steps, the chief trotted up. "Looks like you've had a day," he said.

"You could say that," Sullivan said with a snort, feeling the tension trembling through him.

John arched a brow. "Price of fame?"

Sullivan gave a firm nod. "A steep one, sometimes."

"Pity," the chief muttered. "Listen, I've got a cruiser

sticking around for the night to make sure no one comes back."

"Thanks, John. I appreciate that."

The chief cupped Sullivan's shoulder in a strong grip, his stare steady, at the ready. "Call if you need anything."

"I will, thank you," Sullivan said.

The chief headed back down the porch steps and got into his SUV, right as Sullivan's cell phone rang. He saw it was Hayes before he answered. "Is Mason okay?" Sullivan asked by way of greeting. Hayes had been here, at the house, but Sullivan had asked him to take Mason home until all this settled down.

"He's all good," Hayes answered. "Don't worry. He's totally fine and happy to be here with us for dinner. Take the time you need with Clara."

"Thanks, appreciate it, man," Sullivan said, the weight squeezing his chest lifting slightly. "Can I talk to him?"

"Sure. One sec."

There was rustling over the phone line, and then Mason said, "Hi, Sullian."

"Hey, buddy, are you having fun?"

"Yeah, Auntie Maisie is helping me paint dinosaurs."

"Cool," Sullivan said, running a hand through his hair, not enjoying this next part. "Your mama has an upset tummy, but she told me to tell you we'll come get you once she's feeling better, okay?"

"Okay."

The last thing Sullivan wanted to do was lie, but Clara was in no state of mind to see Mason right now. Truth be told, either was Sullivan. The article shook him. The paparazzi had always been cruel, but never like this. They'd taken their story and made it look far worse than the truth of Sullivan's past.

More rustling then Hayes came back to the phone, laughing. "He appears done with you. We've got this. Don't worry." A pause. "How's Clara?"

"Rattled," Sullivan said.

"Anyone would be," Hayes commented. "All right, we'll keep the little dude busy until you guys call."

"I owe you, thanks, Hayes."

"You don't owe me shit." Hayes ended the call before Sullivan could say anything more.

With a sigh, he tucked his phone into his pocket and scanned the property one final time, but didn't see a reporter in sight. Though he did see the police cruiser sitting at the end of the driveway. For years, he'd wanted the fame, the recognition. Now he'd hand it over in a second to avoid the way it hurt Clara. Determined to fix this, he went inside, locking the door behind him, and headed up the staircase. Every step of the way and creak of the wooden floorboard beneath his feet, he swore he'd done the right thing, but he realized his misstep now. He'd brought the reporters right to Clara's doorstep when he gave the press conference to publicize the brewery. And the baseball game only confirmed she meant something to him. He should have known better—should have anticipated they would dig into his connection to her. He'd let his guard down, and he shouldn't have. He'd done this to her by coming back, and he'd hurt her...*again.*

When he reached the bathroom door, he knocked softly. "Clara?"

"Come in."

He opened the door then wished he hadn't. She was in the claw-foot bathtub set against the left wall, full of bubbles. Makeup streaked her cheeks, and he could see the heartbreak written all over her face. *Betrayal,* her eyes screamed at him. "Clara, anything I said in that interview was to protect you and is not how I feel," he told her, closing the distance between them.

Her gaze held his. "I know."

She didn't believe him, and his gut twisted. He knelt by the tub. He explained further, "If they think there is nothing going on here, they'll leave you alone." However, he could tell his words weren't enough and that any headway they'd made was gone. She was guarded again. Not that he could blame her. He knew without even asking what truly scared her. "You're worried about Mason."

She shut her eyes, tension radiating from her. "I've spent his whole life trying to keep him in a safe, happy bubble." Her voice cracked. "They've twisted our story. Took the worst parts of it. Told lies. I don't want Mason hearing any of that. All I wanted to do was protect him, and I've failed at that."

Sullivan breathed past the constricting of his chest. "There is one way to stop them, but you're not going to like it."

She froze, a cold worry filling her eyes. "You have to leave."

Of course, she had already considered this. "It's the only way to stop this." He knew the impact his words would have and saw them ricochet off her face. "To stay here would only have the reporters digging deeper. Hell, they will start loitering around Mason's school. They're vultures. Writing more stories. Let them write that I left you and Mason again, and this will end it. I'll return to Boston and let this die down." He paused to consider, thinking this through from every angle. "I can get a PR company that can help smooth all this out for us."

Clara's brows pinched. "But if you leave now, it's only going to make you look worse."

The bubbles began popping as he stroked her warm cheek. "I'm used to looking bad, Clara. I can handle the media's negative attention." He leaned closer, needing no distance between them. "But what I can't handle is how this hurt you and Mason. I'm sorry this happened. I never expected the shit that happened in Boston to follow me here."

"Who could have expected it?" Clara asked, tugging at her damp hair. "I just hate how they twisted our story."

"It's part of the deal, and sadly, I'm on their radar right now." Heady emotion filled her eyes before she shut them and leaned her head back against the tub. He couldn't take the silence. "Please tell me what you're thinking."

"I hate how they portrayed everything." She opened her red eyes, tears rimming them. "They only took the bad, without any of the important parts...the stuff that makes our story...*ours.*"

Desperate to take this all away so the pain didn't touch her, he stroked her cheek again. "That's what they do. They create a narrative and roll with it. People, sadly, enjoy hearing about the bad."

"I don't know why," she said, a single tear sliding down her cheek. "It's awful, and it's our past, and no one has any right telling it." She shut her eyes again and took in a shuddering breath. "I'm very worried about Mason."

Sullivan felt the pain ripple through his body. He'd done this. He reached into the bath and took her hand, squeezing tight. "I won't let them get to Mason again. Clara, look at me." She opened her eyes again, and he added, "They won't get to him. I swear it."

"You can't stop them, Sullivan. They've already twisted

the story enough that the kids at school are going to torment him. He was so proud you played baseball. Now, they're going to tell him you never wanted him." Her voice broke. "It's so cruel."

It occurred to him then that her greatest fear had come true, and so had his. His involvement in her and Mason's life had fucked everything up. "I'll make this better," he said, unsure how at the moment. "I'll do whatever I have to do to distract them, to get them off your back. And then I'll come back to Mason...to you, and we'll put this all behind him."

She cocked her head, gave him a measured look. "Don't do anything stupid that will get you another suspension."

He'd come here to get over his suspension. To get back into the game. To fix his life. He cupped Clara's face. "The last thing I'm going to do is stir up more trouble. I'm going to get them off your back, nothing more."

Her chin quivered. "When are you leaving?"

Not wanting to answer, he rose and grabbed a facecloth off the shelves next to the pedestal sink with the vintage mirror above. When he returned to her, he dipped the face-cloth in the water then began cleaning the makeup off her face. "Now."

She visibly swallowed and gave a slow, disbelieving shake of her head. "So, this is all the time we've got?"

His chest constricted at the truth in front of him. When could he come back? At what point would it be safe? How could they manage all this and Mason? He and Clara were better, but they needed more time. "I'm sorry, Clara, hurting you and Mason, and leaving you like this, wasn't what I wanted at all."

"I know," she said, rising, bathwater splashing as she climbed onto his lap. He wrapped his arms around her warm, sudsy flesh. She smelled of lavender as she met his lips with a kiss that made his mind go utterly blank. Until she whispered against his lips, "Once more, Sullivan. Please, I need you once more before you leave."

He heard it in her voice then. She believed he was leaving her again. For good. Unsure how to make all this right, and feeling desperation to keep her close and safe, he wrapped his arms around her, holding her tight, and sealed his mouth across hers. He kissed her feverishly, until they were both breathless and she was grinding against him. There was a time to tease, but this wasn't that time. All he wanted was her, and he knew she wanted the same.

Leaving his clothes in place, he grabbed a condom from his wallet out of his back pocket, and she rose up enough for him to open his jeans. When he settled the condom in place, he didn't wait. He wrapped a hand around her hip and lowered her down onto him. Their groans echoed in the bathroom as she began moving, rocking back and forth, their mouths and tongues dancing together until they had a rhythm that wasn't about a release; it was about a connection. He felt tied to her, grounded by their history and the affection between them.

She moved faster, harder, and Sullivan leaned away. He cupped her face, held her gaze as she rode him. Lost in her eyes, he realized he knew exactly how to show her he had no intention of leaving her like he did before. That this time, it was different. That he would come back. "I love you, Clara," he said, and she froze atop him, her eyes wide in surprise. She slid her delicate hands through his hair, and he knew now, more than ever, he had to tell her. "I have never loved anyone before you, and there was no one after you. Just you. Always you, Clara."

She leaned in, and he thought she planned to end the

conversation with a kiss. Instead, she surprised him by saying, "I love you, too, Sullivan."

Needing to hold onto her, he tangled his fingers into her hair, holding her tight. "I'm going to make this safe and right for you and Mason. I'm going to fix all this. We will figure this out, and when I come back, we'll be the family we should have always been, Clara."

There was a flash in her eyes, the slight look of familiarity to know they'd been in this exact spot before. "Promise?" she asked. The exact same words she asked him seven years ago.

"Promise," he told her firmly. He couldn't stand that look of doubt on her face. Hated himself for it. He wished he could go back and change everything, but he couldn't. All he had was now, and he wouldn't waste it.

Gathering her in his arms, he gently laid her out on the bathmat. On his knees, with her love sweetening the air around him, he hooked her legs on his arms and, staring into that perfect love, wanting to stay there forever, drove into her. Claiming what he wished he could keep with him always, he took them both where they wanted to go. Together.

14

L ater that night, a few hours after Sullivan said a gut-wrenching goodbye to Mason, Clara stood outside of her son's door watching him sleep. She felt like it was impossible to draw in air into her lungs fully; everything felt empty. The way his eyes saddened when Sullivan said he had to leave to go home to play baseball caused Clara's chest to ache, but with the promise of Face-Timing tomorrow, Mason had simply hugged Sullivan then run off to play. Alongside that, *I love you, Clara,* echoed in her heart. A month ago, she'd been determined to not let Sullivan back into her heart. To say goodbye at the end of his time here, able to put the mistakes of the past behind her. Now she didn't want to say goodbye. This time, his leaving felt different, of course, but it also felt as wrong as the last time. He should be here, with them. All this pain, all the heartache. They both deserved a win. More importantly, Sullivan deserved to stop being on the receiving end of abuse, and as far as Clara was concerned, the reporters, telling their lies and spreading hate, were equally as abusive.

Clara sighed, folding her arms to warm the chill in her veins, and leaned against the doorframe, listening to Mason's soft snores filling the room. When the coast was clear, she'd picked him up from Maisie's, and her sister came back to the house with them. Even now, she could hear her sisters talking in her bedroom. From the beginning, all Clara had wanted to do was protect Mason. But she'd allowed her heart to open to Sullivan again. And just like before, he was gone, and all that was left was Mason and her and her heart that was hurting tonight. Unsure of her next steps, she shut the door a little then headed for her bedroom.

The moment she entered the room, Amelia, sitting against the pillows on the headboard, asked, "Do you think Sullivan will come back?"

Clara laughed softly, closing the door a little in case Mason woke up and heard them talking. "Been dying to ask that?"

"Yes," Amelia said with a firm nod, playing with the loose strands on the quilt on her bed. "So, do you?"

Clara pondered, feeling like she was right back where she'd been the last time. Only this time, Sullivan's leaving felt worse. Hurt more. "I want to say yes."

"But you don't think that's true?" Maisie asked from her spot on the end of the bed.

"I think it's complicated," Clara explained, moving to sit with them on the bed. "I think he'll do what he thinks is right. And right now, staying away is better. He wants to protect us. That's his nature. He did it before, and he'll do the same thing now."

"Ah, I see," Maisie stated like she knew it all.

Clara felt like she knew nothing. She frowned at her youngest sister. "Ah, I see, what?"

She blinked, as if she hadn't meant to say that out loud. "Oh, nothing." She quickly set her gaze everywhere but on Clara.

Not going to happen. Clara reached forward and gave Maisie a pinch on her arm. "Spill it."

"Ow," Maisie muttered, rubbing her arm. She exchanged a long look with Amelia then said, "Okay, well, don't rip my head off, but I mean, it seems like you two have fallen back into your old selves. He's running from anything that's hard. You're letting him because you're too afraid to be another person who makes his life hard. But the reality is that you want him to stay. And I bet money he wants to stay too."

Clara stared blankly at her sister. "Please tell me how you got that from anything I said?" she asked in all seriousness.

Amelia cringed and lifted her hand. "Don't kill me either, but she's not the only one who thinks that."

Clara looked between her sisters. "What is this? Gang-up-on-Clara time?"

"Not ganging up," Amelia countered, giving a don't-shoot-the-messenger look, still fiddling with that piece of string. "But we're just pointing out that you don't need to be the strong, responsible one all the time. To make sure everything is perfect and nothing goes wrong. Shit, Clara, things might fall apart completely, but that's okay because sometimes good comes from that."

Fine and all, but... "Do I need to remind you that I am the responsible sister in this family, the one who makes sure things don't fall apart? It's who I am."

"No, you don't need to remind us. Believe me, we are all very aware," Amelia said with a sly smile as she took Clara's hand. "We're lucky to have you to make sure everything runs so smoothly, but I think that this side of you became even more...um, prominent...after Sullivan left and you had Mason. Like, you're so scared of things getting out of control, because the last time they were, you were left heartbroken."

She wasn't wrong. "So, what exactly are you getting at?" Clara asked, trying to understand.

"Stop pretending," Maisie stated matter-of-factly, as if that explained everything.

"Stop pretending?" Clara repeated.

Maisie gave a firm nod, taking Clara's other hand. "Stop telling yourself you don't need him and want him in your life. Stop pretending your heart doesn't want him to stay, no matter how hard it gets. Stop pretending Sullivan isn't your one and only. Just stop pretending, Clara, no matter the fallout."

Clara stared at Maisie, absorbing those words until she realized they sounded all too familiar. "Oh, my God," she breathed, wiggling out of her sister's hold. She leaned over to reach into her nightstand and took out the letter from Pops.

"What's that?" Maisie asked.

Clara unfolded the wrinkled letter that had been opened a thousand times before. "When Pops passed away, he left me a letter with a quote on it." She glanced at her sisters. "I'm guessing you all got quotes too?" At their nods, Clara continued. "I never understood the quote he left me before. But now, I think I actually do."

Amelia leaned forward, peeking at the paper. "What's the quote?"

Clara read the note. "We are what we pretend to be, so we must be careful what we pretend to be."

"Holy shit," Maisie breathed.

Amelia's eyes were huge, and her hands covered her mouth. "He knew..."

Clara stared down at the paper, a warmth sliding through her heart that felt like a tight hug from Pops. All this time, he had known what she could never see. "I—"

Maisie's cell phone beeped, halting Clara. Maisie grabbed her cell off the nightstand and winced. "It's another article." Her gaze, full of pity, lifted to Clara. You don't want to see this."

"Yeah, right, like that's going to happen." Clara snatched up the phone, and her blood boiled at the article: SULLIVAN KEENE, BREAKING HEARTS ALL OVER THE COUNTRY. HOW MANY MORE SECRET CHILDREN DOES HE HAVE?

"These people are vicious," Clara growled her frustrations. She tossed the phone onto the bed, staring into Amelia's eyes and then Maisie's, feeling like the world was slipping away from her. How dare these damn reporters? She'd had the love of her life ripped away from her once because of Sullivan's father. And now, these strangers were doing the same damn thing?

"Uh oh," Amelia breathed.

"Ah, Clara," Maisie said, as Clara's nostrils flared. "Are you okay?"

"Am I okay?" she asked, more to herself than anyone else. For years, she thought she was okay. She thought she had everything handled and had shoved all her feelings away to always put Mason first. She was sick and tired of shoving everything down. Now she let what she wanted... what her heart wanted to rise up. And with her heart's needs ahead of her mind's logic, she knew exactly what to do now, and with Pops' final piece of advice in her heart, she didn't even question herself as she headed for the bedroom door.

Amelia called after her. "Clara, wait, where are you going?"

Clara kept on walking, hot anger burning with each step.

"To stop this damn cycle and take matters into my own hands." She stopped at the doorway and glanced over her shoulder. "Maisie, can you stay and watch Mason?"

"Of course, yeah," she said, cautiously. "I don't need to worry though, right? You're not going to get yourself arrested for punching anyone?"

Clara couldn't stop the bubble of laughter that rose up. She did have a history of that. "No, I'm not going to punch anyone. Promise." She set her gaze on Amelia, who grinned from ear to ear. "I need you to come with me."

Her sister hopped off the bed and rubbed her hands together. "I love when you get like this."

"Like what?" Clara asked, heading down the staircase.

Amelia snicked. "Pissed off."

Sullivan had regrets piled on top of regrets. He'd done many things wrong in the past. He'd run away once from River Rock then spent years running from the memories of his life here. This time, while his reasoning for leaving was different, he was still running. Nothing about that sat right. Questions battered his mind. *Is this the right thing to do? Should I stay and fight, or will that only hurt Clara and Mason?* And that's what it all came down to; he simply couldn't risk either of them being hurt because of his past reckless behavior. His actions had put him on the paparazzi's radar, and only he could get those reporters out of River Rock.

Needing a drink more than ever, Sullivan arrived at Kinky Spurs, where a young man, with rolled-up sleeves, who barely looked old enough to drink replaced Megan. The place was packed full of people playing darts, eating dinner, or kicking back with a drink. The tables and booths were crowded, full of patrons laughing with friends and enjoying the football game on the TV affixed to the wall. Sullivan's stomach rumbled at the scent of grease coming from the kitchen, but what he needed more was a stiff drink. He headed for the bar, where two thirty-something men sat at the far end, arguing over a football game. He took the other end, sitting on the hard wooden stool butting up against a brass foot rail. He kept his head down, not wanting to make eye contact and invite anyone over for an auto-graph. Some would still come, but he hoped they could read his mood.

When Sullivan slid onto the stool, he said to the barkeep who'd made his way over to him, "Two shots of whiskey."

"Coming right up," the barkeep said, tossing a towel over his shoulder, leaving a trail of cloying cologne in his wake.

The country music was upbeat and much appreciated. The last thing Sullivan needed was some depressing song to make him forget the reason he had to leave. The bartender set his shots down in front of Sullivan right as his cell phone beeped in his pocket. "Thanks," he said, then grabbed his phone, finding a text from Marco: GOT YOU A PRIVATE FLIGHT TONIGHT OUT OF DENVER. LEAVING AT 8:00 P.M. IT'LL BE GOOD TO HAVE YOU HOME.

Sullivan replied: APPRECIATE IT. TALK SOON.

With his gut twisting, he set his phone down to reach for the first shot when a familiar voice said from behind him, "So, you're leaving again, huh?"

Sullivan polished off the shot then glanced over at Hayes, who slid onto the stool beside him while Beckett took the other side of Hayes. "How'd you even know I was here?" he asked.

"I'll take a Foxy Diva," Hayes said to the barkeep, a request echoed by Beckett. When Hayes glanced at Sullivan again, his mouth twitched. "Have you forgotten that this is a small town and everyone knows everyone's business?"

Sullivan snorted. "Apparently, too much of people's business."

The barkeep delivered the beers, setting them in front of Hayes and Beckett. "Let me know if you want seconds."

"Thanks," Hayes told him.

A long moment passed while Sullivan stared down into the dark amber liquid of the whiskey in his shot. He appreciated the loud conversation, the clanking of glasses, the whirl of the blender, the noise. Silence would be the enemy now.

"Are we going to talk about the article?" Beckett asked. Sullivan looked his way, and Beckett grimly added, "It's shitty, what that reporter printed."

"That's putting it lightly," Sullivan countered, barely controlling the hot rage bubbling up. Only this time, he knew better. With two shots, he'd stay sober. He'd think clearly. Anything more than that would get him in trouble. "That article already hurt Clara and will hurt Mason too."

"Maybe," Hayes countered, with his wise eyes watching Sullivan all too closely. "But it's not your fault these pricks found out about your past with Clara and twisted it all up."

"It's my fault for coming back," Sullivan said, reaching for his other shot, ready to numb the unforgiving ache in his chest. "It's my fault for stupidly holding a press conference at the brewery and getting them into the game. I thought I was helping..." He slammed back the shot, embracing the burning deep in his throat. "They're going to twist the narrative on what happened with Mason. And he will be hurt."

"Then, beat them to the punch and tell *your* story," Beckett said, spinning his bottle between his fingers.

"It's not that easy," Sullivan said, wishing everything

were different. Wishing his damn life were different. Simpler. "Nothing about any of this is easy. These reporters are vultures. They'll invade this town, and you know the locals; they'll talk. They'll learn about my father...about it all, and in the end, Clara and Mason's lives will be left in tatters because I brought these pricks around."

Hayes sighed heavily and agreed, "It is a difficult situation, no doubt about that."

"Exactly," Sullivan said. He paused as the barkeep dragged his damp rag across the bar, in front of him. Only when he moved away did Sullivan add, "I need to get these fucking reporters away from here, and the only way to do that is to leave." At Beckett's snort, Sullivan glared sideways. "You think I'm making a mistake?"

"I think you made a mistake when you left last time," Beckett said without any hesitation, giving a flippant stare. "This time, I think you're a damn fool."

Sullivan arched a slow eyebrow. "A fool?"

"A damn fool," Beckett shot back, fire in his eyes. "You've got a second chance here to right a serious wrong from the past. To make Clara happy. To give Mason the dad you once had then lost. If I were you, I'd fight like hell to make that happen, not run away. *Again*."

Sullivan felt his jaw tighten, and he unclenched his jaw, not to lash out at a friend. A good friend, in fact. He held Beckett's hard stare, and it occurred to Sullivan then that Beckett wasn't only offering advice but speaking from his loss of Amelia. But they hadn't seen Clara's tears today, the hurt in her eyes that he'd put there, and her belief that, as Mason's mother, she'd failed at protecting Mason from something that could deeply hurt him and leave a lasting imprint on his soul. Sullivan didn't want to cause damage. He didn't want to be a part of the problem. He wanted to watch her and Mason thrive, smile, laugh. "History is repeating itself all over again," he said with a weight on his chest. "I hurt her, and it's fucking killing me."

A pause. A long, heavy pause.

Then, "I know you think all is lost," Hayes said, cupping Sullivan's shoulder with a strong hold. "But there's got to be a way to fix all this that doesn't involve you leaving."

"Besides," Beckett said with a smirk. "If River Rock does one thing well, it's protecting the people who live here. We just need to get on top of this."

They made it all seem so simple. Sullivan arched an eyebrow. "Any ideas on how to do that?"

Before anyone could come up with a response, the bar's door opened and Clara headed in with Amelia in tow. Sullivan whirled around on his stool right as Clara closed the distance with a fast-paced speed and grabbed two fistfuls of his shirt. "Don't go. Stay. Here in River Rock, with me and Mason. I want you in our lives. I want to be your wife. I want you to be Mason's father. I want forever."

Sullivan sensed the crowd go still around him. The music faded. The noise gone. Only Clara remained, and each demand she made hit him straight in the chest. "I want those things too, Clara, but how?"

Determination glowed in her pretty eyes. Her voice was steady, lower pitched. "Well, first, stop running away and face this. I heard one of the reporter's from earlier is currently working at the coffee shop. So, let's go talk to her. Let's tell our story. Our way. Our truth."

He cupped her warm cheek. "What if that hurts you and Mason?"

"It won't," she said, lifting her chin, adamant. "It can't. You know why?"

"Why?"

"Because it's the past, and it no longer hurts me. We wouldn't be *us* if we hadn't been through what we've been through. I'm tired of pretending. All of it happened, the good, the bad, and the awful, but somehow we came out of it all better people. I'm really proud of that. Aren't you?"

Damn. He loved this woman. "I am proud of us."

"Good," she said, firmly. "Then, let's go tell our story. No more hiding. No more pretending. Let's put it all out there so the only story out there is *our story.*"

Hayes, Beckett, and Amelia closed in around them—his chosen family—and he felt all the shame of his life melt away, surrounded by so much love. "Let's tell our story. Our way. Our truth."

15

When Clara and Sullivan entered the coffee shop, she found the space nearly empty, but she spotted the wives of the Blackshaw brothers—Harper, Megan, and Emma—chit-chatting over dessert in a booth by the large window overlooking downtown. The barista stood behind the counter stacked with chrome espresso and frothing machines. Freshly brewed coffee infused the air, alongside the tingle of spices. Clara gave the Blackshaw wives a quick wave, which they returned, but she stayed focused on the woman sitting at the booth near the window. She was a cute twenty-something girl with long brown hair, black glasses, and bright-colored lipstick. Clara remembered her from when the reporters had showed up at the house earlier.

"We got this," Sullivan said, next to her, obviously sensing her slight hesitation.

"Yeah, we do," she said, taking his outreached hand. She was taking Pops' advice to heart, and now that she knew what he meant, it all seemed very simple. The truth had to end this. They got lucky that they'd found any of the reporters, but small towns were good for keeping tabs on people. One visit to the local B&B, and Clara had learned the reporters came to the coffee shop often. The reporter's head was down, her fingers flying over her keyboard, likely writing a story on Clara and Sullivan's life. Determined to put a stop to this for good, Clara sidled up to the booth. "Hi," she said by way of greeting. "I'm Clara Carter, but I'm guessing you already know that."

The reporter glanced up, her eyes going wide, her face losing some color.

Clara heard Amelia ordering dessert behind them, as she gestured at Sullivan, "And as you know, this is Sullivan Keene."

The reporter finally blinked. "Um, hello, yes, I do know who you both are." She drew in a sharp breath then seemed to collect herself. "I'm Mindy Sommers."

Sullivan stepped in closer, wrapping a protective arm around Clara's waist. "Well, Mindy Sommers, we've got a story for you. Do you mind if we sit to tell it to you?"

Mindy's gaze suddenly scanned the area, obviously looking for some sign that this was a joke or a mistake. When she settled her gaze on Clara again, she said, "Er, no, I don't mind."

"Great." Clara slid into the booth, Sullivan next to her. The radio station played soft rock in the background as Clara drew in a big deep breath and blew it out slowly. Pops was right—she was sick of pretending. Her past, no matter how messy and complicated, was hers, and that past had shaped her into who she was today. "Yes, Sullivan left me, but I was the one who never told him he had a son."

Someone's fork clanged against a plate. Clara glanced up to see the Blackshaw wives sitting statue-still. She waited for the instant regret of speaking her biggest moment of shame aloud, but it never came. "I'd like to tell you our story, and I'd like you to print it. This will be an exclusive."

Mindy looked as frozen as everyone else seemed in the coffee shop. "Okay," she eventually said, after she clearly processed what she'd heard. "And what do you want from me in exchange?"

Clara had considered this from every angle. "I want to make sure the story reflects that our son, Mason, is loved, not a dark secret from Sullivan's past." Because in all this, Mason still mattered above all else. His mental health. His happiness. She didn't want him to face the heartbreak that she and Sullivan endured. She wanted better for him.

Before Mindy could reply, Sullivan grabbed Clara's hand under the table, bringing it onto his thigh. His palm was clammy, cold. To Mindy, he added, "I trust you'll tell this story exactly as we say it, but in case you don't." He reached into his pocket, took out his cell and opened the Voice Memos, and hit record. "You don't want a lawsuit from me."

Mindy didn't even give the recorder a second look. She reached for her laptop, her fingers hovering over her keyboard. "I'm ready when you are."

The long lump in Clara's throat shifted, the words she never thought she could say aloud, spilling free. "Our son's name is Mason. He's six years old. As you already know, Sullivan and I were high school sweethearts." She sent a smile his way.

His warm smile erased the ache in her heart.

Focusing back on Mindy, she continued, "Thing is, back then, our lives were very complicated. Sullivan's mother died of cancer. It was a long terrible death, which impacted his family. Most importantly, his father. Before her death, his dad was loving, warm, and affectionate. After her death, he struggled with alcoholism. Later, his kidneys shut down."

Her gaze fell to Sullivan again, who watched her closely with adoration glowing in his expression. "But we all knew he died the day Sullivan's mom did. It's just his body took longer to go."

Sullivan swallowed. Hard. His fingers tightened around hers, though his gaze was all for her. Only for *her*.

The words fell easily from her lips because this was her narrative. Her way to tell their story. "Sullivan's father became physically and emotionally abusive. So much so, that Sullivan was taken out of his father's home when he was sixteen years old." Sullivan's jaw muscles clenched and unclenched, but Clara pressed on. "To escape the abuse, he moved away from River Rock to chase his dreams like his mother would have wanted."

Mindy stopped typing and lifted her eyebrows, no judgment on her face, only curiosity. "You couldn't go with him?"

Clara's heart panged as Sullivan gave a pained expression. She simply gave a smile she hoped reassured him. Done with the pain and all that was stolen from them, she spoke the truth. "He didn't want me to go."

"Is that why you never told him about your son?"

"That's a complicated answer," Clara said in all honesty. "First, Sullivan had just left to play for the Red Sox, and I was sad and confused. I wanted to tell him, but I also wanted him to achieve his dream of playing professional baseball. Ultimately, I suspected if I told Sullivan, he would have come home. But I think his father would have sucked every bit of life out of Sullivan until there was nothing left. I chose to keep Mason's identity a secret to protect Mason..."

"From me," Sullivan finished.

Mindy's gaze cut to him. "Because emotionally, you weren't well?"

Sullivan sighed dejectedly then answered with a small

nod. "I haven't been well for a very long time, and my latest suspension clearly shows that, but I'm working on dealing with the trauma from my past and am doing well."

"You're doing amazingly well," Clara said before Mindy could respond. "And we're immensely proud of him. Facing the past is hard. Especially when that past is filled with abuse."

"Thank you." He smiled a smile just for Clara, soft and sweet that spread warmth between them. Obviously not caring Mindy was with them, he cupped her face before planting a gentle kiss on her mouth.

Clara lost herself in the kiss, feeling every bit of his affection he put into it, as well as the cold void when he leaned away. Wanting to melt into him and get wrapped up in his arms, but also needing to finish what she'd started here, she said to Mindy, "Life is messy. It's good and bad and sometimes really ugly. Sadly for us, we had to deal with really ugly when we weren't old enough or mature enough to deal with that. We made choices. Hard ones. And we've lived with those choices, but now I know, we did what we thought was best, and all those choices came from love."

"Deep love," Sullivan agreed, his soft features implying a calmness she'd never seen before on his face.

For that alone, Clara would have told this story a thousand times over to a thousand reporters. Now she knew that Sullivan needed to face his story completely, as much as she needed to not let him run. The damage his father had placed on Sullivan was melting away before her eyes, slowly replaced by only the warm love his mother gave him.

"Wow," Mindy breathed slowly, leaning back in her seat and wiping a tear off her face. Her gaze flicked between Clara and Sullivan before she shook her head. "Just wow."

She looked at her laptop's screen for a moment, cleared away a few more tears.

Confused, Clara glanced at Sullivan. He just shrugged.

The ding of the cash registers followed the shuttering sound of the till tape paper printing before Mindy finally closed her laptop and set it aside. "I'm not this horrible paparazzi reporter who wants to ruin either of your lives. I'm just out of school, needed a job and some writing experience, and this is where I ended up."

"Okay," said Clara, having no idea where Mindy was going with this.

She pressed her hand against her chest, her fingers splayed out. "Your story is really touching. Complicated and emotional, but even I can see all the love in there. So, I promise I'll write just what you told me and make sure to keep your son's best interests in mind."

Sullivan lifted an eyebrow. "And your editor will agree to that?"

"I'll get her to agree," Mindy said, speaking into the recorder like she had nothing to hide. "Because some stories need to be told, and yours is one of them."

Heat radiated through Clara's chest as she turned to Sullivan and smiled. "She's right, you know, our story does need to be told."

The noise, the customers, even Mindy disappeared as Sullivan cupped her face, moving closer. "No more hiding. No more pretending. We protect Mason the best we can, but let's move forward. We'll do this, together."

She brought her mouth close to his and promised, "Together."

16

One week had gone by since Sullivan sat next to Clara as she told a version of their story to the reporter in the coffee shop, who later printed the article. An article that bled the truth in all its rawness and had showed all the love between the hard times. The past days had been good ones. Clara and her sisters had decided to sign with Ronnie after getting the exact terms she asked for. And Ronnie had joined in the celebratory dinner, including meeting his nephew for the first time. In the coming months, Foxy Diva would find its way into stores and restaurants throughout North America, and Sullivan had no doubt the success would only continue from there. He'd requested another couple of weeks off from his coach to get things settled in River Rock before returning to Fort Myers, and the request had been granted. In a surprise that he had never seen coming, he received kindness not scrutiny from the article and the press, and the truth was, with Sullivan becoming an instant-family man, the focus had shifted off him and moved on to the next hottest bachelor in baseball who they could get their claws into. But that new family of his was the reason he and Clara were bringing Mason to Sullivan's old childhood home.

After he unlocked the front door, he let Clara and Mason enter the house first.

"I'm checking out back," Mason yelled, running through the house.

"Be careful," Clara called after him.

Sullivan stepped farther in, and just the smell, a little dusty but familiar, brought Sullivan back to good memories with his mother and his father before everything changed. He tried hard to think of the *before*, remembering the good, not the bad, as Elizabeth had taught him. He decided to stay in therapy, and when he couldn't see her at her office in River Rock, they planned to talk over Zoom. He moved down the hallway where shattered family pictures and memories once lay. Now all of that was gone. He entered the living room with the big bay window on the front that had once displayed flowered curtains, but now lay empty. The only thing left was the old brown carpet. And even that needed to go.

Clara sidled up next to him, wrapping her arms around his waist. He gathered her in his arms as she said, "After your dad passed away, I sold all the furniture in an estate auction. I figured, even if you came back, you wouldn't want the money, so I put it all in Mason's education fund."

He kissed the top of her head. "That was exactly the right thing to do with the money."

"But I did keep some of your mother's things. We can pull those boxes from the attic."

"I'd like that." He scanned the space, finding the living room much smaller than he remembered, but a little paint and new hardwood floors would help brighten up the space.

Clara tipped her head back, hitting him with those warm eyes. "Is it weird being back here?"

"No, not weird," he said, releasing the breath he hadn't known he was holding. "It's just a house now." He glanced around the dirty walls with peeling wallpaper. "But there are memories here, and many of those memories are good." Christmas mornings. Easter dinners. So much happiness when his mother had been with them. Her smile was what he remembered the most.

"It's good you have those memories," Clara said, offering her captivating smile. "I have so many good memories in this house too."

"I'm glad you do," he said, dropping his mouth to hers.

The kiss didn't last. Mason came barreling back into the living room. Before he took off again, Sullivan kept Clara close but said to Mason, "So, buddy, we've got a question for you." When Mason stopped bouncing around the room, he set those clever eyes on Sullivan. "What would you think about moving in here, with me, after we fix it up? You can even help paint your bedroom."

Mason's eyes widened, a big smile filling his face. Until he frowned. "What about Auntie Amelia?"

"She'll be okay," Clara said, stepping out of Sullivan's hold. "She's getting married soon, to Luka, remember? They're going to want their own space, and Luka will move in with her at the brewery." When she went to Mason and knelt in front of him, his forehead wrinkled. Clara took both his hands. "This is your choice, sweetie. If you don't like it here or it doesn't make you happy, we can stay with Auntie Amelia and figure out the rest later."

Sullivan would live with Amelia and Luka if he had to, all to make Mason adjust to this new life with Sullivan in it.

Mason nibbled his bottom lip then glanced at Sullivan. "You'll live here too, with me and Mama?"

Following Clara's lead, Sullivan joined Clara and took a knee next to Mason, cupping his shoulder. "I'd like to, if that's okay with you."

Mason looked between Sullivan and Clara. A couple of times. He rocked back on his heels, and his smile beamed. "That's okay with me."

"Good stuff," Sullivan said, giving Mason a quick high five. But that was only half the reason Sullivan brought Mason and Clara here today. He gave Mason a little nudge on his arm. "Remember, just like we talked about." When Clara looked on with confusion, Sullivan explained, "Mason and I were talking earlier today, and we both decided our family should be a little more official than it is."

Mason took the ring box from his pocket, and as he held it up, he exclaimed, "Mama, let's get married!"

Clara jumped to her feet, her hands covering her mouth, tears welling in her eyes.

Determined to get this next step in his life right, Sullivan took the ring from the box and held it up to her. "I loved you the day I met you, Slugger. It took a few years, but I finally found my way back to you. Nothing would make me happier than for you to be my wife. Will you marry me, Clara?"

"Yes," she cried, dropping her hands. "Yes, of course."

His wife. Sullivan felt a new purpose wash over him—one to always make her happy—as she slid the princess-cut diamond ring on her finger, a perfect fit. "I love you, Clara," he told her, his voice rough to his own ears.

She smiled through the tears. "I love you, too."

Overwhelmed by this life she'd given him, he gathered her in his arms, and his lips sealed over hers.

"Ew," Mason said, proceeding to make gagging noises.

Sullivan laughed against Clara's mouth then reached out to tickle Mason's side, sending him into a fit of laughter.

When that laughter ceased, Mason looked up between Clara and Sullivan, swaying from side to side. "So, does this mean I can call you Dad now?"

Sullivan froze.

Clara laughed softly at whatever crossed Sullivan's expression and wrapped her arm around Mason, pulling him into her. "Sweetie, you can call Sullivan whatever makes you happy."

Mason wiggled out from Clara's hold. His clever eyes searched Sullivan's and then he said, "I like Dad. I'll call you that."

Sullivan felt his throat tighten. He gathered Mason—*his son*—in his arms and hugged him tightly, even if he was obviously too big for hugs from parents. "I'd like that too, buddy."

Mason withstood the hug for a couple of seconds before tearing away and took off, running down the hallway. "What room is mine?" he called.

"The one on the left," Sullivan answered. His old bedroom.

Mason ducked inside the room. A moment later, "Cool," came from inside.

Clara's eyes were laughing as she looked Sullivan's way. "Isn't it amazing how kids deal with things adults would have a breakdown over?"

Sullivan nodded. "He's a good kid, and all credit goes to his incredible mother." He grabbed Clara by the belt loop of her jeans and pulled her into him, holding her close. This time, he kissed her with the deep love that only came from two souls who'd gone through hard times and found their way back to each other.

When she eventually leaned away, she smiled up at him. "What are you thinking about?"

"How much I love you," he said.

She smiled big. "I love you too, but there's something more. I can see the wheels in your mind turning."

He held her tightly, staring down at this woman who gave him a life he hadn't known he needed. "Oh, I was just thinking about how I left this house, never intending to return. But I want to make this home a happy place again, something I think my father wished for when he left the house to you."

"I think so too," Clara said.

"That would make my mom very happy too," he said, no longer keeping those thoughts to himself. "There's love in this house again."

Clara kissed him once more. "And there always will be."

EPILOGUE

For as long as Clara could remember, she'd had her wedding planned. From the flowers decorating the barn, to the linens on the tables, to the dance floor, where the guests would laugh and celebrate her marriage. Only, this beautiful wedding she'd dreamed of wasn't hers.

Amelia wore a gorgeous, fitted mermaid gown with a long veil that was currently covering her face. Just seeing her, Clara's heart hurt a little that their parents or grand-parents weren't there to see Amelia get married. A week after Sullivan proposed, they were married in a small cere-mony with friends and family in the backyard, under the big tree. In the end, she hadn't wanted a big show. She'd only wanted Sullivan and those who had been there for them through it all. Except Sullivan had invited a few teammates and his agent. The day had been perfect, and somehow, even though their lives had once been very complicated, the last year of their life had been easy. They lived in Fort Myers for the summer months when Mason didn't have school and Clara worked remotely. When he was in school, Sullivan lived in River Rock as long as he could, and they traveled to see each other as often as possible. Sure, it wasn't conventional, but it was perfectly theirs. And at some point, Sullivan would retire from baseball and come home for good. When he spoke of his future, it involved a plan to coach for the University of Denver, bringing up new ballplayers into the major leagues.

When the violinist began playing, indicating the ceremony was about to begin, Clara squatted down and said to Mason, who looked cute in his dress shorts, white shirt, and bow tie. "Remember, all you have to do is walk down the aisle with the rings on the pillow, hand them to Luka, then go sit on Dad's lap, okay?"

"Got it," Mason said.

This kid amazed her. He'd been more resilient than even Clara thought possible. He seemed so happy to have Sullivan in his life—they really were two peas in a pod— that the whys and hows of why Sullivan hadn't been there before really didn't matter to him. Those hard questions would come, but Clara knew she and Sullivan would be ready for them. Together.

She straightened his bow tie. "I'll be right behind you."

"Okay," Mason said.

"Ready?"

He nodded. "Yup."

She kissed his cheek. "Okay, go on, then."

"Ew." He wiped off her kiss before doing nothing she'd told him to do. Instead of walking, he ran nearly the whole way then stopped and talked to a few people before going to sit with Sullivan.

She sighed back at Maisie. "Well, he got down there and the rings are still on the pillow. I guess that's a win?"

"I thought that was going to go far worse, to be honest,"

said Maisie with a laugh, striding by and walking down the aisle in her light purple bridesmaid's dress.

With Maisie on her way, Clara turned around to Amelia. "Ready?"

Amelia visibly swallowed, looking a little doe-eyed.

Clara had been there. Even with today being the happiest day of Amelia's life, being the center of attention wasn't easy for any of the Carter sisters. She took Amelia's clammy hands in hers and squeezed tight. "You've got this. Trust me, the ceremony is the hardest part. After that, we party. Okay?"

Amelia exhaled slowly then nodded. "Okay. I'm ready."

"Yes, you are," Clara said with a smile. "I'll see you down there." And because there wasn't a father figure to walk her down the aisle and tell Amelia the things a father would say, she added, "You look absolutely beautiful today, Amelia."

"Thank you, Clara. I love you." And this time, she looked a little more like herself.

"I love you too." She gave her sister a tight hug then faced the guests again. Thinking of their family who wasn't here today, and loving them instead of sadly missing them, Clara made her way down the aisle. Her gaze skipped past everyone to Sullivan sitting in the front row with Mason on his lap. His smile made her heart flutter. Would always make her heart flutter.

The violinist, who was stationed off to the side of the groomsmen, switched to a different song when Clara settled in next to Maisie. When Amelia began walking down the aisle and the guests rose to greet her, Clara spotted the moment when Amelia's gaze drifted to Beckett, who stood next to Hayes, before she snapped her eyes back on her future husband.

Amelia had gone back and forth about inviting Beckett

to the wedding, but in the end, it seemed wrong not to have him there. Even if they had a lot of history between them, they were still friends. Good friends. And, of course, Beckett still loved her madly, only Amelia failed to acknowledge that. But their time had passed, even Clara knew that.

Time slowed a little as Amelia settled into her spot in front of Luka. Clara got a good look at him then, finding Luka a little pale, she had to withhold her snort. Of course he'd be the type to faint. She didn't like Luka and still thought Amelia deserved better, but this choice wasn't hers.

The officiant began, "Today, we're here to celebrate—"

"Wait."

All eyes went to Luka.

He sputtered something incoherent then said to Amelia, "I can't...I'm sorry, Amelia. I can't do this."

Gasps echoed in the barn. Loud voices filled the silence. The crowd slowly beginning to rise from their chairs.

The officiant looked on in horror as Amelia threw up her veil. "What?" she snapped.

Luka glanced back at his parents and his grandmother, who all looked like they'd seen the same ghost. "I'm sorry," he told them, his skin ashen. "I got wrapped up in it all. I—" His gaze fell to Amelia's. "I'm sorry. I can't go through with this. I don't love you anymore."

Luka stumbled and turned to run away, only he didn't get far.

Beckett leapt up from his seat and punched Luka dead center in the face, sending him soaring backward to land hard on the ground.

Maisie sighed, leaning over to Clara, and said, "Now *this,* this I expected."

Clara's heart broke for Amelia, who began crying. Her

dream wedding, her perfect life, crashing around her as she took off running out the side door.

Sullivan was there a second later. "Go. I've got Mason. Go."

He did have Mason, and they had each other. "I know you have us both," she said, and his warm smile hit her right in the heart. She gave him a quick kiss then ran after Amelia, with Maisie in tow. With each and every click of her heels against the cement floor, she knew the exact advice she was going to give Amelia—life can be messy. It can be scary. It never goes how you want it to. But somehow, in all of it, there is love. All you need to do is look in the right place to find it.

ABOUT THE AUTHOR

Stacey Kennedy is a *USA Today* bestselling author who writes contemporary romances full of heat, heart, and happily ever afters. With over 50 titles published, her books have hit Amazon, B&N, and Apple Books bestseller lists.

Stacey lives with her husband and two children in south-western Ontario—in a city that's just as charming as any of the small towns she creates. Most days, you'll find her enjoying the outdoors with her family or venturing into the forest with her horse, Priya. Stacey's just as happy curled up indoors, where she writes surrounded by her lazy dogs. She believes that sexy books about hot cowboys or alpha heroes can fix any bad day. But wine and chocolate help too.

ACKNOWLEDGMENTS

To my husband, my children, bestie, family, and friends, it's easy to write about love when there is so much love around me. Big thanks to my readers for your friendship and your support; my editor, Lexi, and my copy editor, Monica, who made this book happen through a very hard time in my life and supported me through many missed deadlines; my agent, Jessica, for always having my back; Regina, for the amazing cover; the kick-ass authors in my sprint group for their endless advice and support. Thank you.

KEEP READING FOR THE NEXT BOOK IN THE THREE CHICKS BREWERY SERIES:

DIRTY GINGER

CHAPTER 1

Two weeks later...

At a little after nine o'clock in the morning, Amelia stepped out of the Uber, feeling like a different woman than the one whose life abruptly took a rattling sharp left into the trash fourteen days ago. "Thanks," she said to the driver, who had already gotten her luggage out of the trunk.

"Take care," the driver replied before getting back in his car and driving away.

Amelia faced the big, white, colonial-style farmhouse located in the small town of River Rock, in the gorgeous Colorado countryside, before she began climbing the porch steps. The house always held so much life. First, when her grandmother and her pops took her, along with her two sisters, in to raise them after their parents died in a car crash. Then when she lived in the house with Clara, Maisie, and Mason after their grandparents passed away. But now, as she opened the front door, she only met silence. Gone were her grandparents. Gone was Maisie. She had moved in with Hayes. Gone was Clara and Mason, living with Sullivan. Within the heavy silence lived the reminder that Luka had planned to move in here with Amelia. Now it was only her.

Refusing to allow the embarrassment and unbearable sadness to fill her again, she slammed the door shut on those thoughts. Literally. When she'd boarded the flight for their honeymoon to Saint Lucia the morning after Luka broke off their wedding, she'd done so with the intention of running away. Only, the lush forests, sunny skies, and the delicious rum for a whole two weeks had pulled her out of her despair and forced her to recognize a couple truths. She couldn't run any longer, and she had to face the fact that Luka hadn't been totally wrong – even she had doubts about their marriage. So she allowed herself three days of hiding in the hotel room dying of embarrassment and grieving the loss of the life she thought she was going to have with Luka before she spent the rest of her trip figuring out her new normal, thinking about what went wrong. But when she'd landed late last night and fell into the Denver airport hotel's bed, she decided that, now that she was back home, she'd have an open heart and an open mind, no more bitterness or shame.

Determined to pick up the pieces of her life, she set her suitcase down by the big wooden staircase, where a gallery of framed photographs displaying happy family moments hung. She took her cell phone from her purse and then headed back outside, approaching the brewery. She only reached the barn's double doors when she heard gravel crunching against tires. A quick look back revealed a big black truck with Rocky Mountain Beer Distribution written on the door.

The truck stopped, and Ronnie Keene exited with an unusually soft smile. He was a couple inches taller than

Amelia and had light green eyes that always looked hard, serious in a way that unnerved Amelia most days. She wasn't a businesswoman like Clara, who usually dealt with Ronnie. He wore a Red Sox baseball cap overtop his bald head, supporting his nephew, Sullivan, who played for the team. But that smile as he approached, that soft, pitying smile, was all for Amelia.

"Good morning, Ronnie," she said, chipper. "Thanks for coming to meet me." She'd sent him the text on the drive back from Denver this morning, wanting to keep busy today. Especially since he'd sent her an email asking for a meeting with her as soon as she felt ready to have one.

"Mornin'," he said, shoving his hands in his pockets when he reached her. "Are you sure you're up to this meeting? Like I said in my text, we can wait—"

"I'm up for it," she said, giving him a bright smile in the hope of easing his worries. "I've spent two weeks relaxing, being spoiled rotten, and having fun. I feel refreshed and rejuvenated and totally ready to get back to work."

Ronnie gave her a nod and looked upon her with something akin to pride. "Clara was saying you went on a trip."

Amelia nodded. "To Saint Lucia." What she thought would be two weeks to sulk had turned into fourteen days of healing. She'd even had some fun. "The trip was exactly what I needed, so please, truly, let's get back to work."

Another nod. "All right, then." He waved out toward the brewery. "Let's get back to work."

Good. One person had accepted her healed heart. Now she needed to get the rest of the nosy, overbearing town to get onboard too. She unlocked the barn doors, whisking them open, and her heart broke a little bit more. She'd had four batches of beer fermenting that she should have checked before leaving for the airport. She had intended to give instructions to her sisters to care for the beer while she was gone, but that had been the last thing on her mind. She could smell the rancid grain the second she walked through the doors. The state of her brewery was terrible, and that fell on Amelia's shoulders. "Ronnie, I apologize for this. Clara and Maisie don't know this part of the business, and I just left—"

"Don't," Ronnie said firmly behind her. "You don't need to apologize." He stepped in next to her and gave a reassuring smile. "I've got no doubt you'll get things up and running again and will meet all your quotas."

"Thanks for understanding," she said, leading him through the brewery into the back storage room to show him all wasn't a total bust. "We will definitely hit the quotas for this month."

Ronnie stepped into the room, scanned the already bottled cases of Foxy Diva, their top selling beer that Ronnie and his distribution company had recently picked up to distribute into every bar, restaurant, and store in North America. A huge feat for a small brewery owned by three sisters. "You always have this much stock on hand?" he asked, looking back at her with wide eyes.

She nodded. "I always make sure I'm ahead of the game." She didn't know what it said about her that she always planned for the worst. A result of losing her parents in a car crash and having her heart broken twice. She knew to stay ahead when things were good, because things always got bad again.

"This is good, Amelia," Ronnie said, turning in a circle. "Very good work." He returned to her, and she shut the storage room's door behind him.

"It won't take me long to get the brewery back in shape,"

she said, trying to breathe shallowly as to not inhale the sour aroma.

"I've got no doubt that's true," Ronnie said, walking next to her down the aisle between the tanks. He stopped at the barn's double doors again, visibly breathing a little deeper now too, crossing his arms. "The reason I sent you the email for the meeting is we had a marketing meeting while you were gone. Foxy Diva is doing well. Really well. But we'd like to draw more interest for the brewery next year. The team suggested we put out a special beer each quarter."

Amelia's mouth went dry. "Wow. That's an amazing offer."

Ronnie nodded. "It's something we've seen work very well with another brewery we've got. The only hitch is we've only got one spot for this type of distribution and three breweries in our roster competing for the spot." He paused, pressing his lips together before continuing, "I realize the pressure this would put on you. If you're not ready, or up for it—"

"I'm up for it," Amelia sputtered before even considering it. Maisie had made their little brewery successful in the beginning by traveling to beer festivals and getting their name out there. Clara was the very reason Ronnie picked up Foxy Diva and distributed it. Now Amelia needed to prove her worth.

Ronnie laughed softly and gave a small nod. "I figured you would be ready." He glanced back into the brewery, tapping a cowboy boot against the ground. "Take a couple months. Brew six different ale samples. After that, we'll run some tastings and see what four come out as the leading contenders."

"Totally doable." Amelia smiled, her pulse racing over

the idea of creating some new beers. She hadn't stretched her mind this way since she took Pops' home brew recipe and adjusted the ingredients, turning the beer into Foxy Diva. Yet at the same time, the little voice in her head worried that she couldn't take on such a huge undertaking. Six beer samples on a sound mind was hard, and her mind felt... shaky. "Thank you for your trust is our product, Ronnie."

"No thanks required," he said. That pride was back in his eyes. "You're a talented brew master, Amelia. You've got a good thing here. Don't forget that, without your talent, the brewery would not be where it is today."

Leaving her speechless at his kind words, he strode away. Ronnie rarely offered praise, and she knew it came from trying to boost her confidence after it had been so publicly depleted. Appreciating his kindness regardless of his reasons, she waved as he drove away. Then with the heaviest sigh of her life, she faced the tanks. Never in her life had she ever left her brewery in this condition. Her teacher, Graham Neal, would drop dead if he set foot in her brewery. "*Sanitize. Sanitize. Sanitize.*" had been his motto. Dust was in places it shouldn't exist. A tank was left open, obviously one of her sisters wanted to clean it and then changed their minds. Likely Maisie.

"You're home."

Startled at the smooth, low voice behind her, Amelia whirled around and found the last person she thought she'd see today. Beckett stood between the double doors, looking as hard as ever. Not only his muscular frame either, but his eyes. Not that she blamed him. Beckett's childhood was no walk in the park, and he wore those scars. "What are you doing here?" Her voice came out snappier than she intended, and she quickly softened her voice, "Sorry, I mean, I wasn't expecting you."

He didn't seem affected and lifted a lazy shoulder. "I've been keeping an eye on your place and saw a truck in the driveway. Came to check it out, but then saw it was Ronnie." He entered the barn, then scrunched his face and backed out. "Did something die in here?"

She nodded with misery. "Yeah, beer did."

"Now that's a damn shame," he said with a familiar half-smile. One she'd seen through all their years together. One she once thought she'd see every day for the rest of her life.

"Yeah, it is a shame," she agreed, leaving the barn doors open, hoping to let the space air out a bit before cleaning began.

"How was Saint Lucia?" he asked, stepping into stride with her, heading back toward his massive dark grey Ford F-150 parked near the house.

"Stunning," she answered. "The nature trails were out of this world. Beautiful hiking. Gorgeous weather. The place is so lush and alive."

"From what I saw, it looked it."

She slid her gaze to him, studying his expression. He avoided her gaze. It occurred to her she shouldn't have been so surprised he'd looked into where she went. Beckett was always the protector, including punching Luka when he'd wronged her.

Their breakup hadn't been because there wasn't love between them. Beckett was three years older, and before Amelia left for college, it became clear the direction of their lives had changed. While she'd cried many tears when Beckett ended the relationship, once she got to Denver for college, a whole new world opened up. Six months after she and Beckett ended things, she'd met Luka, and throughout her time at school, they eventually fell in love. When she finally returned to River Rock, the love for Beckett remained, only it was a different kind of love. Not so needy and desperate, but more familiar and comfortable – a very good friendship. No matter what, Beckett was there for her. Always. And she was there for him too when she could, though he was terrible at asking for help.

When they reached his truck, she faced him again. "Thanks for keeping an eye on the place while I was gone. I really appreciate it." She paused, realizing she had something else to thank him for. "And thanks for punching Luka in the face. I had definitely wanted to do that, but didn't have the mind to actually make it happen."

"You never have to thank me for that. I'll happily knock him out on your behalf anytime you'd like." His mouth twitched as he tucked his thumbs into the pockets of his jeans. "And as for your house, it's on the way to the farm, which I really need to get to."

Warmth carried through her, and she smiled as he headed for his truck and got into the driver's seat. Beckett had once been on his way to becoming a professional calf roper, but instead he now worked for Nash Blackshaw, who owned a horse training facility that rehabilitated troubled or young horses. The facility was a well-known staple in Colorado now. People came from all over the country to buy horses from the once famous bull rider, Nash Blackshaw. Beckett was a part of that, and Amelia always liked the special connection he had to horses and was happy he found his place in the world.

Once inside his truck, he rolled down the window and gave her face a long look with his strong gaze. "The trip looks good on you."

"Thanks," she said. "The trip felt good on me, too."

His soft smile made her smile too. "Good to have you home, Am." Only Beckett called her that nickname, reminding her of easier times when life was a whole lot simpler. He flashed her his charming grin that had once been all she could think about before he drove away, a trail of dust following his truck.

She waited until the truck vanished up the road before she let the daunting reality hit her. She had very little time to come up with one new sample, let alone six. Some of the darker ales had to ferment for five weeks, meaning she needed to get on her plan pronto. Sure, she'd been playing with a handful of new brews over the last year, but when Ronnie's company picked up Foxy Diva and put the beer into circulation, Amelia's focus had been getting ahead of supply and demand. But first she needed to deal with the messy state of her brewery. The rest she'd figure out later. Pushing the rising tension— that had all but evaporated in the tropics— away, she entered the house and shut the door behind her. The silence. It was everywhere and it was heavy, a reminder that her sisters' lives had moved on, and hers...

She shook her head, not allowing her thoughts to take her to that dark place. This was her new normal, and she had to move on.

Moving into the kitchen, she smiled at the tulips in the vase on the old, work oak kitchen table. The table held so many memories. Some good. Some bad. All family meetings, hard or otherwise, happened at the kitchen table. The spot had always been a safe place. A quick look in the fridge revealed it had all been cleaned out sometime since she'd been gone. That hadn't been Beckett. This was her sisters' touch. And as unsteady as things were, her family wasn't an issue. They were her rock.

A knock on the door came seconds before it opened, and her younger cousin, Penelope, called, "Amelia?"

"I'm in here," Amelia replied.

Penelope had moved to River Rock two Christmases ago and never left. Amelia was happy for it. Penelope handled the brewery tours that came in every weekend and knocked them out of the park. She'd learned the ins and outs of the brewery in record time, and she could now explain the beer making process without pause and answered every question flawlessly. Most of all, she was incredible with the public. People loved Penelope. Amelia could see why, she loved Penelope too.

When Penelope entered the kitchen, she looked as gorgeous as ever. Her long brown hair was perfectly in place and her green eyes were sparkling with happiness. Amelia was glad to see it too. Penelope's horrible parents had shipped her off to live with Amelia and her sisters every summer at their grandparents so they could *enjoy* their summers traveling without her. Nevertheless, Penelope had created a good life in River Rock, and she deserved every little bit of happiness that came her way.

"Oh, girl, your tan is to die for," Penelope said, opening her arms wide.

Amelia walked straight into them, holding her cousin tight. "It's easy to get tanned when all you do is drink your face off by the pool bar."

"Nice," Darryl, Penelope's husband, said, entering the kitchen carrying two brown paper grocery bags. Scruffy-bearded, with dark brown-hair, Darryl was a cop with the local police department, and his amber eyes, while kind, held authority too.

Amelia studied the grocery bags, pressing her hand to her chest. "You brought me groceries?"

He set the groceries down on the kitchen counter. "Clara asked if we could pick you up necessities. She and Sullivan had a meeting with the principal this morning." Darryl threw Amelia a smile over his shoulder. "Mason got into a fight."

"Uh oh," Amelia muttered, only imagining how Clara reacted to that news. Likely not well.

Penelope laughed softly. "I've never seen Sullivan look so proud. Mason was just standing up to a bully."

Darryl began pulling the groceries out of the paper bags and setting them on the counter. "Sullivan's convinced he'll be a ball player, but I'm betting my money on him becoming a cop one day." At Penelope's nod of agreement, he turned his attention to Amelia, giving his serious look. "And you? How are ya?"

"Good." When they both just stared at her, she laughed to break the silence. "Honestly, I'm in a good place. I spent three days crying in my hotel room, hiding under the bedsheets, and ordering room service. But the trip was exactly what I needed, and I'm glad everything is over. I don't have to see or hear about Luka again, and life can carry on." Or at least that's what she would keep telling herself until she believed it.

Darryl cringed.

Penelope looked at everything but Amelia.

"What am I missing?" Amelia demanded.

Penelope and Darryl exchanged a long look before Darryl asked, "You haven't heard about Beckett?"

Amelia frowned at them. "I heard that he was watching the place for me while I was gone, but that's it."

"You haven't seen him?" Darryl asked.

Amelia looked from Penelope to Darryl, and her frown deepened. "He was just here, but didn't say anything. What's going on?"

Darryl set the basket of strawberries down, then turned

to face Amelia, giving her his serious cop look. "Luka pressed charges against Beckett."

Amelia blinked. Processed. Heat tingled in her face. "You are kidding me, right?"

Darryl slowly shook his head, clenching his jaw. "I'm afraid I'm not, and Luka's not dropping the charges either. I've spoken to him on two occasions to follow up to see if he had changed his mind. He hasn't."

Amelia could barely believe what she was hearing, a tremor rocking her to her core. She gripped the counter tight. "Wait. Luka is really charging Beckett for a punch to the nose? Which he rightly deserved?"

Penelope gave a quick nod, taking out the bananas from the grocery bag. "I guess Beckett broke it real good. Luka's health insurance covered the original break, but there's a bump on his nose now. Luka needs plastic surgery to correct it since it's not covered."

Amelia couldn't wrap her head around this, wanting to help put away the groceries, but feeling rooted to the spot. "What is Beckett facing here?"

"Luka is suing him for the money to cover the surgery. But Beckett will also face third degree assault, which is a Class 1 Misdemeanor," Darryl explained. "It could get him two years in jail and fines up to five thousand dollars."

A sick feeling sank into her stomach as the realization dawned on her. "This isn't the first time Beckett's had that charge." It happened after his twenty-first birthday. The judge had considered Beckett's clean history and he had ended up with probation and mandatory counselling.

"I know, that's the problem," Darryl said solemnly.

Penelope said, "Last time, they let him off easy because he was a first-time offender with a clean record. This time, it's not going to happen again, because to a judge, it looks like he has a history of violence."

Amelia pondered all this, and it all boiled down to one conclusion. "I need to go talk to Luka."

Darryl gave a grave nod. Though he didn't seem happy about it, he said, "Looks like it might be the only way to get him to change his mind."

Amelia drew in a long breath, processing everything that had happened since she got out of her Uber this morning. "Let me get this straight. I need to get the brewery cleaned, come up with six new beers as per Ronnie's request this morning, and mend things with my ex-fiancé that dumped me at the altar in order to save my ex-boyfriend from jail time."

Penelope smirked. "Welcome home."